HUNKER DOWN WITH THE MCKALLISTERS

A CAKE SERIES BOOK

J. BENGTSSON

This book is dedicated to the year 2020.
You know what you've done.

CONTENTS

MCKALLISTER FAMILY TREE

Scott McKallister (Patriarch)
married to
Michelle McKallister (Matriarch)

Children
Son **Keith McKallister** (Married to Samantha Anderson)
Wyatt and Thomas

Daughter **Emma McKallister** (Married to Finn Perry)
Indiana, Kimi, and Paige

Son **Jake McKallister** (Married to Casey Caldwell)
Miles, Slater, and Lily

Son **Kyle McKallister** (Married to Kenzie Williams)
Arlo and Axel

Son **Quinn McKallister**

Daughter **Grace McKallister**

Mitch McKallister (Married to Kate Mullens)- Scott's son from previous relationship

*For additional Cake series family trees (including the in-laws) go to my website > jbengtssonbooks.com
Family Trees courtesy of Shanelle Bridgeforth

PROLOGUE: JAKE MCKALLISTER
INSTAGRAM VIDEO

I KNOW THERE'S A LOT OF INFORMATION CIRCULATING ABOUT THE coronavirus. I was away for a few weeks in an area later designated as a hotspot, and upon my return to Los Angeles went into quarantine and was tested for the virus. The results came back this morning, and I tested positive. My symptoms are mild, and I'm being virtually monitored from my family's home. My brother Kyle was with me during the time I was away and has also tested positive, so we're riding this out together.

Since returning home, neither of us has had any physical contact with our wives or kids. Our main priority is to keep from passing this virus on to anyone else, so we'll be following the rules and guidelines laid out for us by the CDC. We'll post periodically to let you know how we're doing. In the meantime, please be careful out there.

JAKE
QUARANTINE – DAY 3

THE VIDEO SHUT OFF, AND I SWATTED KYLE'S FINGER AWAY from my ear.

"My god, Kyle. Did you really just give me a wet willy during a public service announcement about the coronavirus? Where the whole point is we're not supposed to be sharing bodily fluids?"

"What does it matter now?" He shrugged. "We're already both infected."

"It matters to me... and to my millions of followers."

"Okay, yeah." Kyle rolled his eyes, putting his hands up to placate me. "I forgot how super important you are. I'll try to keep my respiratory droplets in check from now on."

Kyle and I had been stuck in the guesthouse at my parents' place since arriving back in the States and, although it had only been three days, he was already getting on my very last nerve.

"I need you over in that corner," I protested, pointing to the furthest away spot in the living room. "Away from me."

Openly defying my order, Kyle plopped himself down on

the couch and crossed his feet on the coffee table. "There are no rules in quarantine."

"That's literally the definition of quarantine, Kyle." My voice rose to an unmanly pitch. "Lots and lots of rules to follow."

"Like what?"

"Like number one – your saliva has to remain in your body. Number two – when I'm in the bathroom, do not pass notes under the door. I can hear just fine. Number three – we both have to agree on a show before bingeing the series. I refuse to get sucked into one more season of *Frankie and Grace*."

"Hold up," Kyle interrupted. "Do I get to add to these rules?"

"No."

"Why not?"

"Because, Kyle, birth order applies to quarantines, which makes me your boss."

"Well, then if we apply the same theory, that makes me the bratty kid brother... and your worst nightmare."

2

FINN

"YOU READY FOR THIS?" I ASKED, GLANCING OVER AT EMMA.

Our eyes met, and for the quickest second, fear cycled through hers. I'd been seeing that look a lot lately, and not just when she left for work. I saw it when she backed away from a hug or as she watched the girls sleep. This was Emma's worst nightmare; her reason for not wanting children in the first place. She couldn't protect those she loved from the virus. But damned if she didn't try.

"I'm ready," she confirmed with a brave nod.

And she was. Covered head to toe in protective gear, Emma was taking no chances. An ER nurse, she'd been on the front lines since the whole pandemic started and had an appreciation for the destruction it waged. A germaphobe her whole life, Emma seemed uniquely attuned to the challenges of battling an unseen enemy.

"Put your gloves and mask on," she instructed.

"I don't need all that." I waved off the protection.

"Yes, you do, because if you accidentally bring something home to the girls, I'll castrate you."

"And I'm putting on the mask and gloves."

A nervous laugh passed between us as I slipped the mask over my face and squeezed around the nose to make a seal.

"I feel like I'm about to exorcise demons."

"Appropriate," Emma chuckled. "Because this is my definition of hell."

She wasn't that far off, I thought, as I pulled my car through the gates of Perryland.

———

KIDS RAN ten deep alongside my car as we made our way down the long driveway. The 'six feet apart' rule apparently did not apply in this rural section of the world.

"I'd ask where their parents are in a pandemic, but..."

"Well, technically, Emma, they are adhering to the stay-at-home order."

"This is true."

We got a spot a few rows back in the makeshift parking lot, which had grown substantially since the lockdown forced my relatives off the streets. Shelby came out of the house wearing only a t-shirt that reached to her knees and a pair of fluffy red slippers. She waved her arms in the air like she was being freed in a hostage exchange.

Emma and I glanced at one another.

"Is Shelby surrendering or something?" she asked.

"If she is, am I required to accept it?"

Emma exited the car, and I was right behind her.

Shelby took a step back. "Oh wow," she said. "Were you two vacationing in Chernobyl?"

"In this day and age," Emma patiently explained, "you

can never be too careful."

"Well, yes, I agree if you're shoveling radioactive waste, but I hardly think a hazmat suit is necessary when visiting the in-laws."

I didn't even need to look at Emma to know what she was thinking. A nuclear meltdown had nothing on the Perrys.

My brother Rocky appeared in the doorway, his body leaning against the frame. With his signature lazy drawl, he fashion-shamed our mother. "Mom, go put some pants on. Jesus."

"If I don't have anyone to impress," Shelby sassed back. "What's the point?"

"The point is I feel like shit, and seeing you half-naked is only making the nausea worse."

He stopped talking as he got a closer look at Emma and me. "You two look like a condom commercial."

"Rocky," Emma admonished. "I told you to go to a room and isolate yourself until I got here."

"Right, but what you might have overlooked was the fact that half the county's population lives in this house. There's no self-isolating. Besides, thanks to Finn, I've spent the last week with these people, so I'm hardly the epicenter of this outbreak."

My brother glared at me like I was to blame for his current predicament. Hey, I'd never asked Rocky to stay. That had been his decision alone. Yes, I'd requested him to look in on Shelby and Gigi after it became clear that neither one of them was capable of surviving this outbreak on their own, but that was a far cry from asking him to book a one-way ticket to crazy town.

And, besides, it wasn't like I'd just abandoned him. I

mean, now that my filming schedule had been canceled until further notice, I'd have done the job myself, but with Emma working all the time, my dance card was filled with a different type of difficult female – daughters.

I fought back. "Rocky, I believe your exact words were, 'I might as well move in until this all blows over, so the kids and me aren't stuck in a small apartment for a month.'"

"And, Finn, I believe your exact words were, 'Please, I'm such a whiny-ass bitch, I need help.'"

Emma broke up the festivities by guiding Rocky back into the house. He'd never been one to follow direction, but with Emma, it was different. He respected her like I hadn't seen him respect anyone else. Of course, that had everything to do with the fact that after he was released from prison, she'd been right there by his side helping him get his life back together. Not only did we get Rocky settled into an apartment with his two kids, but I also hooked him up with my agent, who immediately started booking him in television and movie roles calling for buff and gruff bikers or Viking dudes.

"I'm fine, Emma," he protested. "Just a little trouble catching my breath is all. Shelby shouldn't have called you."

"Yes, she should have," Emma said, pointing him to the couch. "You're family."

I caught the barely-there smile that tipped his upper lip and knew what that meant to him. Rocky and I had survived on our own nearly our entire childhood, so I could imagine having a support system was not only comforting to him but also a welcome relief.

While Emma examined Rocky, I got a pinch in the ass from my granny's grabber arm.

"Do you mind?" She aggressively shooed me out of her

line of vision. "It's the Showcase Showdown."

"Oh, sorry," I said, stepping outside of her *Price Is Right* radius. As always, Grandma Gigi was perched in her armchair throne with a pile of treats by her side. "You look like you have everything you need to survive an apocalypse."

"Except Rocky won't buy me my fruit snacks."

"They were out, Grandma," he called to her from the couch. "What did you want me to do, raid the preschool down the street?"

"Besides, Gigi," I said. "Maybe this would be a good time to replace that processed food with the fresh fruits and vegetables that are still plentiful in the stores."

She sighed. "Indy, if I wanted your frou-frou Hollywood opinion, I'd have asked for it."

"Yeah, Indy," Rocky laughed, but the wheezing that accompanied it worried me.

I stood off in the corner mesmerized by the dipshit on the TV who bid a measly $14,000 for a trip to the Bahamas *and* a Chevrolet Blazer and then went on to be rewarded for his stupidity minutes later when the other contestant overbid on her living room package.

"Finn," Emma whispered, pulling me aside. She didn't have to tell me; the look on her face said it all.

"Oh, shit. Not Rocky?"

She nodded. "He has all the symptoms. I'm going to take him to my hospital. You need to seal this place up tight. No one can go in or out."

"How do you propose I do that – with the National Guard?"

"Do whatever you have to do, Finn. Perryland is now closed."

3

EMMA

"MAYBE WE SHOULD CALL AN AMBULANCE," FINN SAID. "I DON'T want you to be exposed any more than you already have been."

"No," I whispered. "They'll take him to the nearest hospital – where no one can visit him. At least at my hospital, I can keep an eye on him. I'll be fine. Look at me – I'm in full cootie cover. It's you I'm worried about. And the girls."

"I'll call Michelle and Scott and tell them what's going on. The girls are fine with them."

And he was right. Finn had moved in over there, caring for Indiana, Kimi, and Paige at my parents' place, where a big backyard and a team of cousins kept the 'shelter in place' orders manageable for everyone. And, with them safely away from me, I could focus on work and not have to worry about dragging something back to the people I loved most in the world.

"Hey," he said, squeezing my gloved hand. "We'll get through this."

Yes, we would; but it was going to take a long and

concerted effort from everyone involved, and that included Finn's super-spreader next of kin, who were about to get the reality check of a lifetime.

———

"How bad is this?" Rocky asked, the crack in his voice speaking to the strain he was under. We hadn't spoken since finally getting him off the property and en route to the hospital. It had been an emotional few minutes, and I knew the toll it had taken on his heart to have to pry his sobbing little girl, Posy, off his leg and then task his stoic nine-year-old son, Nike, with looking after her. It was a predicament no parent would want to go through, but especially not a single parent with no backup plan.

"Listen, you're going to be okay," I answered. "Jake and Kyle are both positive and only came down with mild symptoms. You're young and healthy; no pre-existing conditions. Don't worry."

Although I was worried. Neither of my brothers had presented with the reduced oxygen saturation level that Rocky was showing. The truth was, my brother-in-law was already too sick to check into *Casa Coronavirus* with Jake and Kyle. If his symptoms were as serious as I thought they were, I feared Finn's brother was in for a rough few days ahead.

"Well," Rocky said, hesitating. "I might not be as healthy as you think."

I glanced over. "What do you mean?"

"I'm a smoker."

"Since when?"

"Since, oh, ten years ago. Off and on."

"Rocky. How did I not know this?"

"Because I have to hide it from Finn. He's into that whole healthy living bullshit."

"It's not bullshit, and I wish you'd told me. I could have helped you quit."

"I know." He laid his head back on the seat. "It's just you and Finn... you're so perfect. It's intimidating."

"*You* are intimidated by *us*?" I shook my head, remembering the first time I ever met Rocky and that feeling of being in the presence of a galactic warrior.

"Don't look so surprised, Emma. I'm an ex-con. Not exactly salt-of-the-earth material... not like my flawless brother."

"First, no one is perfect or flawless or whatever other adjectives you've attached to Finn and me. I'm a bundle of nerves. I can be a selfish bitch. And I judge people sight unseen. And Finn... he's... I mean, he's... no, you're right, he's pretty perfect."

"See?" Rocky said. "Exactly my point."

We laughed, but it was short-lived, as Rocky's mood was a somber one. "You aren't selfish, Emma. When I came out of prison, you had every reason to judge me. What you did for me, I'll never forget that. And..." Rocky's voice broke.

"Hey." I gripped his arm. "It's going to be fine."

He recovered straightaway, clearing his voice of any emotion. "If something happens to me, I need you to promise..."

"Rocky, nothing's going to happen."

"If something happens, Emma, promise me that my kids won't grow up with Shelby. I know it's a lot to ask, but I'd want you and Finn to raise Nike and Posy. With you two, they'd have a chance. Please, promise me."

The look on Rocky's face was one I'd never seen before – that desperation. He and Finn had both grown up in squalor, but unlike my husband, who'd been removed from the home as a teenager, Rocky had remained. Whatever hardships he'd suffered in Finn's absence had never been revealed, but I had no doubt his life had been a tough one. I couldn't turn my back on Rocky any more than I could on one of my own brothers.

Meeting his eye, I made him a solemn vow.

"I promise."

4

KYLE

"I FEEL LIKE ONE OF THOSE PROSTITUTES IN THE WINDOW IN Amsterdam," I said as I settled into the chair in front of the large picture window.

Jake dropped down beside me, slapping me on the knee. "You'd be so very lonely."

"Please. I'd have a line around the block."

"Oh," Jake chuckled. "Okay."

"Screw you, dude, I'd make a kick-ass hustler."

"Not in your current condition, you wouldn't."

"Speak for yourself, dickhead. I'm not the one wearing bald eagle slippers."

"They were a gift from my kids. What, am I *not* supposed to wear them?"

"Yes, that's right. You're *not* supposed to wear them. It's common courtesy."

Our argument was cut short when the kids began to gather around the window. Some were dressed in tights, while others just had sweatpants on, but all were barefoot.

"Uh-oh," Jake grinned. "I have a bad feeling about this one."

Every third day, at noon, the Lockdown Kids performed. The ensemble group consisted of all the grandchildren currently sheltering in place at the McKallister house. That included my two sons, Jake's three kids, and the three Perry girls. The first Covid-19 performance had been a rock concert, which Jake and I both wholeheartedly supported. The second show was an unorganized synchronized swimming number, with the little non-swimmers performing their routines in a plastic wading pool.

"Oh man," I laughed. "I think this one's a ballet."

"100% it is. Casey knows I'm not a fan. She's just torturing me."

The music started, and sure enough, the kids began a riveting performance of *Swan Lake*. The only reason I knew that was because some of the kids were wearing homemade duck hats fashioned with felt and pipe cleaners. I noted Kenzie off to the side, her laugh unbridled as she watched the boys entertain. Life on that side of the window was still vibrant and fun. I wanted to be on that side.

Over here in the red-light district, things were stale and uncertain. While Jake basically napped his quarantine away, I spent my days flipping from one news station to the next, filling my head with ever more troubling facts and graphs and curves. The world was going to shit while I was sheltering in place in a luxury pool house. Each day I spent in quarantine was another day of fear and doubt. Would life ever return to normal? Would my kids ever know a world without disease?

Surprisingly, Jake didn't seem affected by the news or by

the virus that continued to devastate. I wondered if maybe he didn't feel fear the way others did. He'd already survived the worst life had to offer, so it made sense that everything after paled in comparison.

"Dad, are you paying attention?" my son Arlo called out in the middle of a pirouette. Arlo had stopped calling me daddy when he was three years old, the age when we both discovered his intelligence far surpassed my own.

I nodded and smiled, watching with surprise as Arlo engaged in the dance with uncharacteristic aplomb. He usually hated movement. Just getting him outside to play could be a challenge. If Arlo was going to kick a ball around, he was analyzing the angles and calculating its distances. When I was his age, if it was round and it moved, I was kicking it into someone's crotch.

School was his sport and, in that, he excelled. Arlo was smart... almost too smart for his own good, and as a result, he spent a lot of time indoors and alone. My firstborn didn't need to be a sports star; I just wanted him to connect, like he was doing now – in a ballet recital. It made me wonder if we'd been focusing him on the wrong activity. Maybe he'd be happier performing in the *Nutcracker* than cracking someone's nuts. Whatever made him happy – that would be the direction I'd point him in. All I asked was for my boys to not feel the need to hide in the shadows – like I'd done for most of my life.

"Daddy, look at me. Look at me, Daddy," Axel hollered, a big toothy grin accompanying my youngest's spastic movements as he flopped on the grass like an earthworm.

Yep, that one was all mine.

"I see you, bud."

Everyone saw Axel. He was life on a giant silver platter.

"He totally doesn't get the point of ballet," Jake laughed.

"No, he wasn't blessed with grace," I agreed, as I watched my mini-me perform.

"This is your punishment for all the years when I'd ask you a question and you'd reply in interpretive dance."

"Yeah," I chuckled. "That was obnoxious. I'm sorry."

"Don't be. Sometimes it was the only laugh I'd get all week."

I wasn't sure how to respond to that. Certainly, it had never felt like a chore to entertain Jake, or to try to lure him out of his tortured head. "Well, I'm glad I could be of service."

"You were more than that, Kyle. I wouldn't have made it through without you," Jake said, the mood in the whorehouse dimming. "You were right to be worried about me. I was on the edge. All I needed was the smallest push and I would've been gone forever. But you were always there, always seeking out attention... like Axel. 'Jake, look at me. Look at me, Jake.' However annoying it was, you never let me look away, Kyle. You wouldn't let me go."

His words sank straight into my soul. We rarely discussed the past. I think the last time might have been at the hospital years ago. As always, I yearned for more, but Jake had already moved on. He was now focused solely on his baby daughter dancing in her mama's arms. Jake adored all his kids, but Lily was special – the little girl he'd always wanted. She'd torn down the last of his defenses and settled herself deep inside his heart.

"Can I ask you something, Jake?"

I could tell by the reluctant way he turned toward me that

he wasn't interested in further discussion, but I needed his wisdom right now.

"Yeah, sure."

"Aren't you scared? The whole world has gone to hell. How are we ever going to get back to what it was?"

There was a long pause before he replied. "We can't go back, Kyle. Life was never meant to be traveled in reverse."

5

FINN

LOCKDOWN – DAY 9

WAS THAT... MY TOILET PAPER?

I looked up at Grandma Gigi's house, which was now covered in long streaks of two-ply gold. Not an inch of the exterior was untouched.

Three hours. I'd left them alone for three hours.

I caught one of the young hooligans by the arm as he raced by.

"What have you done?" I accused.

"We're just playing," the tweener replied. "What's your problem?"

I snatched an intact toilet paper roll from his hand and shook it in his face. "Where are the rest of them?"

"Gone."

Gone? They couldn't be gone. I caught my breath before hollering at the top of my lungs. "Shelby! Bucky! Anyone with kids! Get out here!"

I held tight to the evidence, in one hand the boy with newly shorn locks squirming in my grip, and in the other, the last living roll of toilet paper in the Perry household.

When I'd first sat down with my kinfolk and told them of the state's lockdown protocol, detailing how the virus jumped from one person to another and how they'd all been exposed, most acknowledged the situation. Some even offered to help me disinfect the entire property. But after returning from the great Lysol challenge, I found several of my cousins shaving their children's hair off. Somehow, my halfwit relatives had equated the coronavirus to a lice outbreak.

My first thought was to try and educate them by turning on the nightly news and giving them a dose of reality, but then it occurred to me that if lice was the worst health crisis they could imagine befalling them, then let them believe the little jumping parasites were the villains of this apocalypse. If it kept my family members six feet apart and focused on cleanliness, then I'd accomplished my goal... sort of.

Shelby and a small gathering of adults oozed out of the front door at banana slug speed.

"What are you screaming about?" my mother asked, slapping her hand to her waist.

Wait... what was she wearing? It was like an 80's Jane Fonda workout leotard, complete with knee-high leg warmers. I lost all train of thought.

Shaking my head free of the image, I waved my arm in a half circle, covering the façade of the house. "Look."

"Yes, Indiana Jones, it's a house," Shelby mocked me, smirking at my cousin Mutt like I was this village's idiot.

He spit a wad of chewing tobacco, his blackened teeth exposed in a righteous grin.

"Yes, Shelby," I said as patiently as my impatience would allow. "I know it's a house. But did you happen to catch how the kids chose to decorate it? I mean, are you throwing a coronavirus party I wasn't invited to?"

"What are you babbling about, Indiana Jo...," she stopped mid-sentence as her brain finally caught up to her eyes.

"Oh, my god!" Shelby gasped, nearly falling to her stockinged knees. "What have they done? How are we..."

"...going to wipe our asses?" I finished her sentence. "That's a very good question."

Bucky stepped down off the porch to stare up in wonder. "Where did they get it? I haven't seen toilet paper in a week."

I cringed at the mental picture of how my cousin was dealing with the lack of butt wipe material, but I had more pressing issues at hand. "I'm glad you asked, Bucky. See, I went to the store before the sun rose this morning to be the first one in line to buy the 36-roll 'limited edition' family pack. I also managed to buy eggs, which I can only assume are now splattered all over the picture windows at the back of the house."

"Indy, what are we going to do?" Shelby continued her over-dramatic bit, even hinting at hyperventilation. "This is a catastrophe."

Okay, well, famine in underdeveloped countries was a catastrophe; but I got her drift. It was going to be a long, hard spring without a little squeezable softness between our asscracks. I sighed. This shitshow needed a hero, and as always, it would have to be me – for no other reason than a lack of any other qualified contenders.

"All right, I need all hands on deck – even the kids roaming the plains. Maura, go get some garbage bags. Collin, grab the fruit picker pole from the shed. Shelby..." I hesitated, trying to come up with the least taxing chore possible in hopes she might actually do it. "Hold my keys."

"Look, people," I continued. "If we all work together, we can salvage some of what's been lost. Let's go!"

I looked up from my inspiring pep talk to find – all my relatives still standing there.

"Is there a problem?" I questioned.

"Can we do it after the Ellen DeGeneres show is over?" Uncle Jimmy asked.

"Is it a rerun?"

"Yes."

"Then no."

A collective groan erupted.

"Uh," Mutt cut in. "I ain't got no kids, so I should be exempt."

I blinked at him. "That statement is entirely false, Mutt. What about the one in Utah? Or the one down the street?"

"*Here*, Indy. I meant here – at Perryland."

"Ugh. I can't help people who can't help themselves. If I don't have every human over the age of five out here in three minutes' time, I'm going back to the McKallister mansion, where bidets render toilet paper useless and I don't have to deal with shitheads like you."

For the first time in forever, my family actually listened.

SCOTT

"Hey, Mom? Dad? I'm home."

"Quinn?" Michelle jumped from her chair as he entered the kitchen, backing away slowly. "What are you doing here?"

"Um," Quinn's eyes shifted between the two of us. "I'm not gonna lie. I was hoping for more enthusiasm."

"No, of course I'm happy to see you," she replied, taking another step back.

"Really? Because you're acting like I'm wrapped in explosives."

"It's just... well..." Michelle turned to me. "Help me out, Scott."

"What she's trying to say, son, is that you're dirty."

"I showered this morning," he protested.

"Not that kind of dirty. You're from the outside."

Michelle tagged back in. "Remember when I told you that you either had to come home back in March or not at all?"

"You were being serious?"

"Of course she was. In case you haven't heard, kid, there's a virus out there, killing old, fat guys like me."

"Come on, Dad, you're not that old," Quinn grinned.

"Shut up."

"So, where am I supposed to go?" my youngest son asked. "Do you think the county dump will take me?"

"Doubtful," I chuckled.

"Scott, you're not helping. We need solutions."

"I mean, I suppose we could toss him in with Jake and Kyle."

"We can't do that!" Michelle said, flashing me her Angry Bird eyebrows. "What if Quinn's not infected?"

"Hello, people. I'm right here," Quinn waved. "And just FYI, this is the worst greeting ever."

"I'm sorry, honey," she said. "Your old room is being used by the grandkids. But what if we clean out the craft room for you and put the blow-up bed in there? I'll feed you meals through the door. Two weeks of solitary confinement, and then you'll be good to go."

My youngest son looked from his mom to me, waiting for someone to tell him he was being punked. His choices were either prison or zombie apocalypse. I wouldn't much like those options either, but we were living in different times now... with different rules. And, honestly, I was with Michelle on this one. Quinn was a damn rock star. There was just no telling what that boy might drag in.

"Forget this shit," he said, breaking the tense moment. "I'm going over to Keith and Sam's house. No way would they turn me away. Keith's the dirtiest human I know."

MICHELLE
LOCKDOWN – DAY 10

THE MINUTE QUINN LEFT, I FELT THE WEIGHT OF MY DECISION. How could I turn my back on my own child? "Do you think we were too hard on him?"

"Absolutely not," Scott replied. "We gave him the option of being imprisoned in his own home, and he turned it down. What more could we do?"

"I'm being serious, Scott."

"So am I. Do you realize that we are down to twelve rolls of toilet paper... *in the entire house?* I ran inventory this morning, Michelle; it's not looking good. As much as I'd like to, we just can't afford to support one more asshole."

In our marriage, we'd been opposites from the start. We'd always made it work, but quarantining with the man was testing my patience. I had to keep telling myself that it was a stressful time, and this too would pass. We'd made it through way worse than this; times that would have killed lesser marriages.

"We wouldn't go through so many rolls of toilet paper if

people would start using the bidets Finn put on every toilet in the house last week," I said. "They work amazing."

"Yes, well, unlike yours, my ass doesn't require power washing."

I rolled my eyes. *Patience. Give me patience.* "And unlike you, I won't be wiping mine like a savage come Friday."

"Yeah, yeah. I've got spies out scouring the shelves. We'll find some before then. Anyway, stop feeling bad about Quinn. He's survived this long in the open air; he'll be fine. I mean, did you see that kid's muscles? He's like a germ-fighting super hero."

"Muscles won't protect against this virus, Scott."

"No, but we can't either. He made his choice weeks ago when we asked him to come home and he refused."

"Right – but he was going through that whole virus denial stage. We should've known he'd come home once reality set in. We should've had his room ready for him."

"Woulda, shoulda, coulda. Michelle, our priority now is ourselves. Who's going to suffer if Quinn drags in the Black Plague?"

"Us," I replied.

"That's right. More *me*, probably... but you too."

"Sure, honey." I laughed. He was such a man. I could be four days deep into the stomach flu when he came down with a sniffle and the world would officially end. "Of course, the virus will punish you the most."

"Thank you. That's all I'm saying. Do you feel better now?"

"I do," I said. Scott always did have a way of calming my anxiety. "I love you."

"I love you too. And just remember, Michelle – now is the time for us to be the grownups and to set a good example."

"You're right."

"I always am," he said, before raising his voice to attract the attention of our grandchildren in the other room. "Now, who wants to play some poker?"

8

QUINN
LOCKDOWN – DAY 10

"KEITH?"

The door was slightly ajar, so I pushed it open, only to find Kali's Surf and Skate shop empty of all human life.

"Sam?"

Nothing. This wasn't right. After leaving my parents, I'd texted Keith and he'd directed me here, where he said they were doing work on the shuttered store. But now that I was here, my brother was nowhere to be found. Most people would take one of two approaches to a situation like this. The first would be to venture further into the store and search for clues. The second would be to back slowly out of the door and call the cops.

But if you're me—the youngest boy of five brothers—*you prepare for combat.*

I didn't have long to wait. From behind a rack of clothes, my nephew Thomas was pushed out into the open in his Gerber baby walker, and as he rolled across the floor unattended, I knew I'd just walked head-on into an ambush.

Springing into action, I raced for cover behind the

counter, but it was too late. NERF gun dart pellets began to fly from all directions. My other nephew, the one who could walk and talk, came out from behind the counter and fired at me. Like a superhero, I deflected the pellet shots with my arms as I advanced on my little foe. Wyatt panicked, dropped his weapon, and ran. But, as luck would have it, one of my steps equaled eighteen of his itty-bitty ones, and I easily caught up to him, scooping my kicking and screaming nephew into my arms and blowing raspberries into his neck.

"Drop the boy!" my sister-in-law said, stepping out of the shadows and leveling her weapon at me. Sam was dressed in short shorts, flipflops, and a frilly boho shirt, with braids cascading down the sides of her head. Not exactly the trained assassin I'd been expecting, but no matter. It was what was in her hands that counted.

"Is that what I think it is?" I asked, stepping back with the squirming boy in my arms.

"It is," she confirmed, squinting at me over the top of her toy assault rifle. "A Nerf Ultra One Motorized Blaster, capable of delivering a barrage of squishy darts with quick, pin-point accuracy. And right now, I'm aimed down."

Our eyes met, and mine narrowed. "Oh, you're playing hard ball."

"Sure," she smirked, her eyes traveling south. "If you say so."

Ouch.

I scanned the perimeter, contemplating my options. I could surrender; but then I thought better of it. My adversaries were a surf bunny and two kids in diapers. I liked my chances. But there was still one wild card out there, and he was hiding somewhere in this store.

Keith.

He was known to play dirty. If I were to have any chance of winning, I'd have to fight fire with fire.

Slowly, I lowered Keith's child to his feet and whispered in his ear. "I'll give you a five-dollar bill if you go find your daddy for me right now."

Wyatt's eyes widened. If there was one thing my nephew liked better than sticking his finger up his nose, it was money. This was, after all, the kid who'd asked for a cash box for his third birthday. While most kids his age were playing Legos or ball, Wyatt was busy ringing up groceries on his kid-sized cash register. He had a whole shady shop set up in his house, where he totally overcharged his clients. I should know. I once paid $4 for a plastic lemon.

"Okay," he whispered in that raspy voice I found so damn adorable. "For $5."

Yep. It was a bargain. To get the kid to turn on his old man was worth ten times that much to me.

I slipped him the cash, and as he turned to leave, I grabbed his arm. "Hold on. Hug first."

My nephew wrapped his little arms around me and squeezed tight before he took off toward the back of the store, outing my brother in a matter of seconds... with me right behind.

"Wyatt," Keith complained, scrambling away as boxes went flying. "Come on. We talked about this. You can't take bribes."

But before my brother could fully form that last word, I tackled him to the ground. We struggled for possession of his Longstrike Nerf Modulus Toy Blaster with barrel extension, bipod, and scopes. That was some serious weaponry, but I managed to wrestle it out of his hands with relative ease.

"Uncle," he yelled before I'd even had time to torture him with it. Disappointed, I settled for straddling his waist and slapping him silly.

"I said *uncle*, asshole," he grumbled, worming out from under me. "Jesus, why do you always insist on disrespecting the uncle rule? It's sacred."

"I don't know, Keith. Why do you always insist on rolling over onto your back like a wussy roly-poly?"

"Hey, I'm tired, all right?" Keith said, making excuses for his lackluster fighting skills as he got to his feet in a three-step process—knees, hands, toes.

"Oh, geez, Keith. I'm sorry," I replied with mock pity. "I wouldn't have been so rough with you had I known osteoporosis had already set in."

"Shut up. I'm sleep deprived, and it's slowing me down."

"Oh, okay."

"What?" Keith said defensively. "Do you have any idea how hard it is for two vertical people to sleep in a queen-size bed with one horizonal three-year-old?"

"Okay, all done. No more bickering, boys." Sam stepped in to give me a hug. "I missed you, Quinn. Sorry about pointing a revolver at your head."

"No problem. Surprisingly, that wasn't even the worst welcome I've had today."

"Is it true Dad threatened to throw you into quarantine with the Hardy Boys?" Keith asked.

"Uh-huh. *And* he called me dirty," I said, shaking my head at the memory. "Such a dick."

Sam patted my shoulder. "Well, we don't think you're dirty here..."

"...any more than usual," Keith added.

"Shush." She smacked him. "And you're totally welcome to stay with us... but there's just one little snafu."

"Snafu?" I questioned. "Is that the elephant on Sesame Street?"

"No, that's Snuffleupagus," Sam corrected. "Let me try that again. The problem is, you'll have to sleep on the couch in the playroom."

Keith held up a finger. "AKA—the living room, which is what it was called when we were cool."

"Can't I take one of the rooms?"

"Which one?" Keith asked. "Ours or the boys?"

"Wait... you only have two rooms?"

"Yes. See, unlike you, Quinn, we don't have millions of dollars in the bank to buy you a comfortable guest bedroom."

"Well, shit," I sighed. "I'm going to have to buy you a bigger house."

Keith laughed. "Be my guest."

"Hey," Sam piped in. "I thought you were quarantining with your girl?"

My girl. Yes, that had been the plan. "I was, when staying inside was still just a suggestion. But when the lockdown went into place, we decided she needed to be with her father. Now, I've been alone almost a week, and I've discovered I'm not meant for solitude."

"Ah, that's sad," my sister-in-law replied. "Let me make up the couch, Quinn. It will be fun. Like camping."

I was actually giving her offer some serious consideration when Keith delivered the final blow. "...until Wyatt opens up his store for the breakfast shoppers. That's generally some-where around 5:30am."

"5:30 AM!" I shrieked. "Is he nocturnal?"

"Close," Keith nodded, his eyes drooping. "Very, very close."

"Ah, man. Thanks for the offer, Sam. But I'm going to Emma's. She's already a cesspool of germs... *and* has an empty house. How can that go wrong?"

9

GRACE

LOCKDOWN – DAY 10

Seconds after turning the water off, I heard his voice. Quinn. Why didn't he tell me he was coming? I stuck my head out of the shower door.

"Forget this shit," I heard him say. "I'm going over to Keith and Sam's house. No way would they turn me away. Keith's the dirtiest human I know."

No! Don't leave. I thought, hastily squeezing the water from my dripping hair and wrapping it in a towel before stepping out onto the bathmat. But the instant my foot hit the fluffy rug, the front door slammed shut. Ah, man. Leave it to Quinn to stomp off in a huff. He'd always been the impulsive type.

Grabbing another towel, I held it in front of my naked body as I trotted to the window. Quinn was already opening his car door. No. No. No. When multiple attempts to slide open the window failed, I took to banging on the glass with open palms like a hostage pleading to be set free. But Quinn didn't hear, nor did he see; and, with water pooling around my feet, I watched as he drove away.

"Quinn," I said, shaking my head as I picked up my phone and dialed his number. One ring. Two. "Answer the phone, dude."

My call went to voicemail.

I wasn't letting him go that easily. I was the type of person who always felt happiest when I had the whole herd huddled around me. But right now, half of us were still grazing in the field. With the virus and the fate of everyone's health on the line, I felt an urgency to draw them in. Starting with wayward Quinn.

Letting the towel drop to the ground, I hastily chose my outfit for the day from the garments lying over my chair. These were recycled clothes that had been previously worn but that weren't dirty enough for the laundry bin... or the floor. In the era of coronavirus, minimal effort was the most I was willing to give, and it showed.

It was hard to believe that I'd been home for a little over three weeks now. After my graduate program switched to online learning, there seemed no reason not to travel back to California and hunker in place with my favorite people. I'd learned at a young age never to take family for granted, and that was truer now than ever before. I'd only second-guessed my decision to come home once... okay, maybe twice... but that was all. See, a house full of adults was an entirely different story than a houseful of kids, and when they started outnumbering the adults, that was when the whole second-guessing came into play. And it was why getting Quinn home was so important to me. He'd tip the scale in our favor—another fully formed brain to talk to.

Certainly I couldn't rely on my father for that adult conversation. He was never without his entourage of tiny humans. In fact, his influence on them was just as pronounced as theirs was on him, and I watched as my father's internal clock began to unwind, Benjamin Button style. His voice dropped to kid-friendly levels, and he spent an unfathomable amount of time planning pint-size adventures for his beloved grandchildren. If there was a poker game to be played, he was the dealer. If there was a food fight to be had, he'd be the one to cast the first carrot. And if there was an 80's prom to be attended, he was the one high up on the ladder adding the twirling disco ball to the festivities.

I brushed my unruly hair up into a ponytail and pulled it through the back of a baseball cap before poking my head out the door. All clear. I sighed in relief. See, my parents not only had strict rules for coming into the house, but also strict ones for going out. If I wanted to leave, I'd have to do it undercover.

Sneaking down the stairs, I passed my dad dealing cards in the dining room while teaching Jake's oldest son how to *burp with his whole gut.* Then I passed the kitchen, where my mom and sisters-in-law were deep in conversation about my brothers, Jake and Kyle. No one noticed me slip out the back door, hop in my car, and drive out of the main gate.

Using the Snap Maps to easily pinpoint Quinn's location, I followed him to Keith's surf shop, hoping to lure him back home. But just as I was about ten minutes away, Quinn left the shop, driving northeast and in the direction of Emma's house. Had Keith turned him away too? Poor guy. He had to be extra salty by now. No doubt I had my work cut out for me.

Undeterred, I took the next exit and followed his path. It wasn't until my brother pulled off into a shopping center parking lot that I finally got the guy pinned down. Pulling up next to his car, I donned a mask and went in search of my brother. I found him lurking in the liquor section of a pharmacy.

Hiding behind a display, I disguised my voice and hummed in my best creeper voice. "Ooh, yes, you're just a delicious hunk of man, aren't you? I could drink you right up."

Quinn froze, whiskey bottle in hand, refusing to look my way. Clearly, he thought me a stalker, and I didn't give him any reassurance to believe otherwise.

"You're Quinn McKallister, right?" I continued in my best husky seductress voice. "You want to come home with me? I'll give you a safe word."

"You've got the wrong guy," Quinn replied, replacing the whiskey on the shelf, and I could tell by his body language that he was preparing to bolt.

"I don't think so," I stepped out of the shadows. "Aren't you the guy who thought Pokémon creatures were real way longer than you should have, even asking for the live versions of Charmander and Pikachu for your seventh birthday?"

Quinn turned toward me, recognition dawning on him. A smile slowly spread across his face as he shrugged. "Keith told me there was a Pokémon farm in Bakersfield. I thought they were adoptable, like puppies."

"Oh, I know what you thought. It's all you talked about for months," I said.

Amused, his eyes traveled the length of me. "You look absolutely hideous."

"Thank you. And you look like a hopeless drunk in need of his next fix."

"I'm going to Emma's," he replied, as if that were explanation enough why he needed a bottle of whiskey at his disposal.

"Did Mom and Dad let you out on good behavior?" Quinn asked.

"No, I snuck out."

"Ooh, Gracie's a rebel now. I like it!"

"Let's not get crazy here. I just needed a breather."

"From what?"

"Quarantine. The kids. Dad," I confessed.

"What's wrong with Dad?"

"Nothing. In fact, he's great— having the time of his life playing with the kids. Yesterday he put on the Olympics for them. The Olympics! He built little podiums and everything."

"Damn. I wish he'd put that much effort into us when we were kids," Quinn commented, somewhat off topic.

"Yeah, well, if you'll remember correctly, we were sort of going through a crisis back then. Not to mention he was working two jobs so Mom could stay home with Jake. He didn't really have time for fun."

Quinn nodded, looking to the ground. "I get it. But still, we got screwed."

"It was a different time." I shrugged, not wanting to acknowledge that this was why I was frustrated by Dad's interest in his grandkids. It wasn't the sweetness of the grand gestures that bothered me. It was that he hadn't done them for me... or for Quinn.

Normally, I didn't allow negative thoughts to take over, but there was something about being with Quinn that brought out the nostalgia in me. And while I believed my childhood had made me a stronger person, Quinn had an entirely different outlook. He considered our shared past a crutch, something to lean on and blame in times of trouble.

"I think of it this way," I said, taking a deep breath and committing to my words. "How many people had a childhood like we did? It was definitely a wild ride. And that makes us unique."

"Tell that speech to your little girl self, Grace. She might not have the same opinion."

We stared each other down. With us, no words were really needed. After the kidnapping, we'd leaned on Emma for support, but once she'd gone off to college a year and a half later, and with Mom and Dad busy caring for Jake—and Kyle and Keith—that left me and Quinn to essentially fend for ourselves. And that was what we'd done. It felt like we'd been relying on each other our whole lives.

"I've missed you, Quinn."

"I've missed you too, Gracie-bear," he said, slinging his arm over my shoulder. "You're the whole reason I tried to come home. I wanted to hang with you, but Mom and Dad insisted on imprisoning me."

"No, they didn't," I replied. "They want you home, but they also want to keep everyone safe. If you follow their rules, you can come home, Quinn."

"Uh, yeah," he scoffed. "I don't think so."

"I'll quarantine with you."

"In the craft room?"

"No, in my room—well, not *my* room. I came home before everyone else moved in, and Mom wanted me to have a comfortable, quiet place to study, so she gave me the giant guest room with the kitchenette and the fenced in patio. We could quarantine together there."

"You'd do that?" he asked, and I could see my gesture meant something to him.

"Heck, yeah. We'll have them bring in another bed. During the days, I'll study and you'll do... whatever the hell rock stars do. During the nights, we'll binge watch all the shows we've never seen."

"And in the morning, we'll make *waffles*?" Quinn said, using his best Shrek donkey voice.

"Yeah, sure. Lots of waffles. It'll be fun—like old times."

I could almost see Quinn's mind exploring the possibilities.

"And, the best part is," I said, excitement building as I used every weapon in my arsenal, "Jake and Kyle will be out of isolation soon, and then we can all be together. It'll be like a giant sleepover. What do you say?"

Quinn stood there, his eyes shifting between the bottle of whiskey, which represented endless cleaning at Emma's house, and me—his little sister and best friend. I knew which one he'd choose even before he did.

"I'm down," he said, grabbing an extra bottle off the shelf. "But I'm going to need an extra one of these."

10

JAKE
QUARANTINE – DAY 12

"Wait." Casey squinted into the phone as our Facetime call connected. "What happened to your beard?"

"*Sydney* happened to my beard."

"Uh-oh," she laughed. "What did our adorable niece say to you this time?"

"First she dissed the quality of my stubble by asking where the 'rest of my beard' was. And then, when I tried to explain that it was only five days' worth of growth, she roasted me by saying, 'Oh, it looks like termites got to it while you were sleeping.'"

Casey shook her head, clearly impressed. "Oh, man, Syd's good."

"Then she went in for the kill, telling me fumigators were going to have to come over and 'tent my head' before I'd be let out of quarantine. Yeah, so, long story short, that's why I have no beard."

"Oh, my god, that's awesome. I love that girl," Casey said through a bout of laughter, before catching my disapproving reaction. "I mean, oh, no, Jake, that's terrible."

"Thanks for your support." I grinned.

"But you know, babe, it really is your own fault. You can't let her win like that."

"It's not like I'm trying. She's just got me wrapped around her finger."

"Imagine what it's going to be like when Lily gets old enough to manipulate you. You'll be like a cube of butter left a second too long in the microwave."

"I know. I'm doomed. At least I have the boys to level it out."

"Ah, the boys miss their daddy so much. *I* miss their daddy so much. I just can't wait for this whole thing to be over."

"Me too. It's weird – even though I see you guys through the window every day, I miss you more now than I do on tour."

"This whole thing is weird. I hate that I can't be with you – that I can't kiss you. I hate that I can't fly home to Arizona to see my parents. I worry about you. I worry about them. It's exhausting."

"How are Linda and Dave?"

"They're doing okay. Staying inside for the most part. But Sydney and Riley are bored, and homeschooling is a challenge. You think you have problems with that girl? Imagine trying to help her with algebra."

"Dave's probably spending a lot of time in the bathroom right about now."

Casey nodded. "I'm sure."

"Speaking of the Caldwells," I said, "I talked to Luke yesterday. Business is booming. I swear, this has to be the only time in the history of the world when being a generator salesman is a good thing."

"I know. He can't keep up with the orders."

"I seriously think people have confused the coronavirus with a zombie apocalypse. They're preparing their doomsday bunkers."

"Maybe they're on to something," she said, attempting a half-hearted smile.

I could feel a heaviness coming off Casey, and that worried me. "You okay?" I asked.

She shrugged. "Yeah. I'm just feeling off, I guess."

"Talk to me."

"I have this uneasy feeling in the pit of my stomach. I know we're apart when you travel, but somehow this feels different. Ominous. I've been..." she hesitated before turning away from the screen.

"You've been what, Case?"

"It's nothing. I've just been having nightmares."

A chill rushed through me. "About what? The kids?"

"No, Jake, about you... not coming home to us."

And then it hit me – the weight of what she was saying. "You're having dreams about me dying?"

Her silence was my answer. And although that was the last thing I wanted to hear when I was sick with a potentially deadly virus, I needed to know what was going through her head and how she was coping.

"Tell me."

"I don't want to."

"Casey, just tell me."

Our eyes connected, and I waited.

"We're at your funeral," she began, her voice barely audible. "The kids... they're all lined up. Lily is wearing your baseball cap, the one she loves to steal off your head. Miles is standing there, his bottom lip quivering. He's trying to be so brave for you. And Slater, he's just completely lost it, screaming for his daddy. It's awful. Everyone is crying... but not me. My fists are clenched, and I'm just furious. That isn't how our love story was supposed to end, you know? We fought so hard to be together, and now that we have it all, it's ripped away from us forever."

"It's just a nightmare. Why are you giving it any weight at all?"

"Because it's playing into all my deepest fears."

"You don't need to worry about me," I consoled her. "If there's anyone more uniquely qualified to survive this thing, please point him out."

"*I* know you're a survivor. *You* know you're a survivor." Tears gathered in her eyes. "But does the virus know that? Have you told it you're mine and it can't have you, Jake?"

"Look at me, Casey. I'm tired and rundown, but I'm here and I'm strong where it counts." I tapped my head. "Before you know it, I'll be back at your side, and all this will be behind us. I promise."

She nodded, but appeared unconvinced. "Finn's brother Rocky is sick."

"I know. He's been in the hospital for a few days."

"No, Jake. I just talked to Emma. He's *really* sick."

"Shit. Really?"

"This virus – it creeps up on you. Rocky had been having mild symptoms for about a week before things got bad enough for him to call Emma, and then, a few days after that, he's in the ICU fighting for his life. And then I look at you, someone who's been having mild symptoms for a week... see where my mind is going with this?"

"I see where it's going, yes, but that won't be me," I said. "And it won't be Rocky either. I don't know him well, but I know he's tough. He'll pull through."

"Tell that to all the people who've died. Being 'tough' doesn't exempt you from this virus. If this thing wants you, it'll take you."

"Yeah, well, that's not going to happen to me," I replied, the first flicker of anger jabbing through my calm exterior. "And you know how I know it's not going to happen? Because the universe owes me, Casey. It fucking owes me."

Casey's eyes widened, clearly not expecting my outburst. Hell, I hadn't been expecting my outburst. But this kind of talk pissed me off. I hadn't survived a serial killer only to be taken by a faceless murderer. That wasn't how my story was going to end... how our story was going to end. I deserved to grow old with my beautiful wife. I deserved to watch my kids graduate. I deserved the future Ray Davis had tried to take away from me all those years ago.

"Not going to happen." I repeated stubbornly, more for myself than anyone else.

"Okay," she replied, her voice stronger than before. "That's all I needed to hear."

"Good. And the next dream you'll have about me will have you writhing on your sheets."

"Yes, please. I need a little somethin' somethin'," she grinned. "Hey, where's Kyle?"

"Watching the news in the other room. Why? Do you want to have phone sex?"

"Not in your parents' house, I don't. Go to the back window."

I got up and headed over just as Casey was walking up, dressed in tight workout clothes that clung to every curve. Her dark hair was slicked back into a ponytail, and it was bouncing like it lived a full and happy life.

"I look like crap," she said. "Sorry."

"No, you look hot as hell."

"Okay, well, then it's a good thing you can't smell me."

"I've temporarily lost my sense of smell, which is a good thing since I'm bunking with Kyle."

She smiled, and I could see her fear had been replaced with longing. She was pining for me, and that was just another reason for me to come out of this stronger than before. Stepping up to the window, she spread her fingers and pressed them against the glass.

I followed her lead, my fingers joining hers. Even apart, we were together.

"Thank you for making me feel better," she whispered into the phone. "I'm sorry I doubted you. And you're right. The universe does owe you."

"Actually, I take it back."

"Take what back?" she asked, her face masked in confusion.

"The universe doesn't owe me shit. In fact, it's actively worked against me my whole life. Do you have any idea how many times it's tried to kill me?"

"Don't say things like that, Jake," she replied, her fingers falling from the glass.

"Hey," I called to her. "Come here."

After a moment's consideration, Casey fused our fingers together once more.

"Don't you get it?" I said, leaning my forehead against the window. "I don't need the universe's help anymore. I've got something now that I didn't have then – a reason to breathe."

11

FINN

"Indy?"

The soft voice filtered through my slumber. Resisting its pull, I grumbled something incoherent. Going on nearly two weeks of babysitting my relatives, I was looking the part. Showering had become an 'every-second-or-third-day' thing, and the skin I normally kept razor-smooth for my woman was now under a furry black animal pelt. How easy it would be to drift off to the dark side... but no. If I ever had hope of finding my way back to Emma and the girls, I had to fight the lure of the Perry clan.

Besides, I was needed here. While Rocky was fighting for his life in the hospital, it fell on me to ease the worries of my niece and nephew, who'd spent the past two weeks following me around like shell-shocked rescue pups. Who could blame them? Their lives had been filled with parental abandonment. Then once they got their dad back and life was finally normalizing, a virus threatened to take him away for good.

And now the pressure was on me to give them some

emotional stability. Unlike my girls, who'd never known adversity, Nike and Posy needed constant reassurance. Even bathroom visits were spent entertaining them outside the door. It wasn't until I sat my niece and nephew down and told them if anything happened to their dad, they'd have a home with Emma and me, that their minds were eased... and they allowed me a little room to breathe.

The last thing I wanted to do was think of a life without my brother, but contingency plans had to be made for if the unthinkable occurred. It was what Rocky wanted, and what Emma had promised him in the car ride to the hospital. I didn't have to make such assurances. Rocky was blood. My allegiance was already in place.

Once Rocky fell victim to the virus, other family members followed. Two were treated and released from the hospital, while others showed mild symptoms and only needed to be quarantined. In an effort to isolate the sick, I had two motorhomes—with all the hookups and modern-day conveniences—brought into Perryland, which I had parked in front of the main house.

But, in a surprising turn of events, the healthy family members, including Grandma Gigi and Shelby, abandoned the house altogether for the comforts of luxury mobile living. And now the majority of the Perry clan were crammed into the motorhomes like hamsters crawling all over each other to make room in the wheel.

"Indy?" a voice whispered directly into my ear, as one of my dark curls was lifted off my forehead, stretched taut, and then released like a Slinky back into my face.

I knew who it was. Posy. And I knew what she was doing.

"No," I answered.

"You don't even know what I'm going to ask," she replied, all innocent-like. I knew better. Posy was no longer the sweet, harmless toddler in riot gear. Now my little niece was a sassy ten-year-old with an appetite for destruction—and science was her new weapon. On the surface, it sounded like a positive hobby for a little girl to have, and if she were running experiments on oxygenation or comparing which cheese molded the fastest, I'd be all for her inquisitive mind. But Posy's science was all about static electricity, dissections, and explosions.

"Look." I opened my eyes. "I told you. I'm not buying you any incendiary devices today, and that's final."

"But they have curb-side pickup," she protested.

"Still no."

Posy sighed, acting as if I were being totally unreasonable. "Mentos and soda is harmless," she countered.

"Not when you pour diet soda directly into Mutt's mouth and drop a Mentos in there. He could've exploded, Posy."

"But he didn't."

"But he could have."

"Fine," she huffed. "What do you want me to say? Sorry."

I nodded my head, curls tumbling everywhere. "Yesss! I've been saying that for days."

She waved me off. "Okay, forget about the Mentos. Let's talk about the helium."

"Nooo! No helium either. My god, creature. You scare me. There is no conceivable reason for you to have a canister of helium unless you have some newfound interest in balloon animals."

She sat silently contemplating her answer.

"Posy? What do you need the helium for?"

"It's a surprise."

"See? Those three words coming out of your mouth are truly terrifying. How about you watch some TV?"

"Boring."

"Play some basketball with Nike."

"Boring."

"Set off a nuclear explosion?"

"Now you're talking."

We both laughed. I opened my arms, and she crawled into them. "What am I going to do with you, Dr. Evil?"

She giggled.

"I know you're bored. So am I. How about when this quarantine is over, I enroll you in science camp?"

She tipped her head to look up at me from her reclining position. "What level?"

"What do you mean, what level?"

"I don't want to be stuck at some camp where all we do is watch plants grow. I want to be in the action. Do they have science boot camps?"

"You mean like tossing grenades into greenhouses?"

"Yeah, something like that."

I tickled her side. "You're truly frightening.

"You know what I really want?" she whispered, suddenly sounding shy.

"What?"

"I want to be like you."

"Like me?"

"I want to be an actor."

I ran her words through my head. Of course – it was the perfect solution for her. A way for her to harness all that pent-up energy. "You'd be an amazing actor, Posy."

She lit up. "Really?"

I nodded. "Yes. And I know what to enroll you in this summer."

Posy climbed onto my stomach, using her sticky fingers to mold and manipulate my face.

"Tell me like a robot," she insisted.

"Acting camp," I replied in my best C-3PO voice. "Same one I did when I was a kid."

Suddenly she was bouncing on my very full bladder. "Yes! I'm going to be just like you, only with better hair."

Grabbing her wrists, I tipped her to the side. "Get off me, crazy kid."

Before she could slide off, Posy bent down and kissed me on my nose. "You're my best friend, Indy. I love you."

"I love you too."

"And when my daddy gets better, can I still come and see you all the time?"

"If you don't try blowing me up, sure."

Posy jumped off and ran for the door of the motorhome, turning to me just before exiting. "Oh, yeah, I forgot. Grandma Gigi told me to come get you."

"Okay," I replied, sitting up and rubbing my tired eyes. "What does she want?"

"Shelby's crying... and not just wah-wah crying. Like ugly crying—what nightmares are made of."

Shelby? Crying? Posy's words didn't make any sense. Shelby made others cry, not the other way around. And then it hit me—

Rocky. Something had happened. I shot out of bed and grabbed my phone, expecting to find a message or voicemail from Emma. Nothing. I wasn't sure if I should be relieved or disappointed.

"What is she crying about?" I asked, already sliding my feet through the leg holes in my jeans.

"I don't know, but she hasn't stopped. It's been going on an hour now."

My god. Dehydration had to be setting in. My feet hit the linoleum floor before Posy even finished her sentence.

———

I FOUND my mother sitting atop an upside-down utility bucket, sobbing.

"Shelby? What's wrong?"

"Stop calling me Shelby!" She halted her bawling long enough to snap at me. "I'm your mother."

I took a step back. Technically, yes, she was, but my whole life she'd insisted I call her Shelby. What had changed since we'd parted ways last night, after watching that episode of *Naked and Afraid*?

"I gave birth to you!" she screamed.

In a toilet, I wanted to remind her, but wisely kept that to myself.

"I nurtured you!"

Aside from the few times she'd rolled over on me in her sleep, she'd never really been much of a cuddler.

"And... and...," she sniffled. "I kept you safe from harm."

Well, now—that was just a stretch. She did pull me out of that manhole once, but I'd argue she was the reason I'd fallen into it in the first place. I mean, who rides a bike with an unrestrained baby on her lap?

"I tried, Indy. I really did. I tried to be a mother, but I wasn't cut out for it." The sobbing intensified. What was happening? Had Shelby been possessed by a poltergeist? I glanced at my wide-eyed cousin Bucky, non-verbally insisting he call the exorcist I was sure he, or someone in the family, had on speed dial, but he just shrugged and grabbed another bottle of beer from his utility belt.

Shaking my head, I focused my attention back on Shelby.

"Okay, *Mom*," I said. If placating her meant using her biological title, that was what I'd do. "What's wrong?"

"I want to take it back," she cried, smearing tears with the back of her hand. "I want to take *all* of it back."

"I'm so lost. Can we back up? What started this?"

"You, Indiana Jones... and Rocky. I should have been a better mother to you. And your sisters." She laughed miserably. "Do you know I haven't seen them in over ten years? I'm not even sure how old they are."

My god. The woman was serious. Shelby was... no, my *mother* was showing her first signs of remorse in her forty plus years of life. Who said miracles couldn't happen? I'd been waiting to hear these words my whole life, if only to throw them back in her face. But looking at her tear-streaked cheeks and seeing her so broken changed my mind. Shelby might have been a colossal fuck-up as a parent, but she was my fuck up... and I chose to forgive.

"If you want, I can try and broker a meeting between you and the girls."

Shelby jerked her head up. "You know them?"

"I do. They reached out to me a few years ago. Buttercup

goes by the name Jana now. She's twenty-three. And Leia just turned twenty-one."

Shelby nodded, years of selfish denial catching up with her. "Do you think they would see me?"

"I'm not gonna lie. They have some abandonment issues. But they're curious. I think once Rocky gets better, maybe we should all plan a meeting."

Shelby dropped her head into her hands. "Oh god, Rocky."

Posy, who'd been standing by my side, slid her arm over Shelby's shoulder. "He's going to be okay, Grandma."

"Grandma? I'm too young to be a grandma."

"Yet you are one." I smiled.

Shelby lay her hand to Posy's cheek. "How can you be so sure your daddy will be fine?"

"Because Emma says so, and she's the smartest person *ever*," Posy answered.

"She is pretty smart," Shelby acknowledged, before looking up at me. "You know what I like most about your wife?"

"What?"

"She was able to look past all this." Shelby swept her arm to encompass Perryland. "And all of this." The second pass encompassed her. "And then she looked in there" – Shelby pressed her finger to my heart – "and found gold."

My phone rang, startling us all. Speaking of Emma... it was a Facetime request from her. Shelby and Posy flanked me on either side as I accepted the call.

"Finn, I just got..." her voice cut out.

My blood instantly ran cold. "I can't hear you."

"EMMA!" Shelby hollered in my ear. "WE... CAN'T... HEAR... YOU!"

Posy's face fell, fear etched over her delicate features. "Auntie, is my daddy okay?

Emma smiled. "See for yourself."

And as she turned the camera away, the image filling the screen was of Rocky—alive and awake.

12

JAKE
QUARANTINE – DAY 30

"Look, Jake. You don't have to get mad. All I'm saying is, cults make perfect sense. It's hard to make friends as adults."

My jaw twitched. I'd left this conversation behind like eight minutes ago, but Kyle... oh man, he just kept harping on it. The original conversation had centered around murder hornets, so I wasn't even sure how we'd made the jump to cults in the first place. Although, to be fair, anything my brother had to say nowadays burrowed under my skin, then suffocated and died. Look, I'm not saying Kyle was the most irritating person on the planet, but he'd sure better hope the other guy doesn't die.

"And plus," Kyle continued, "if you put aside the brainwashing, cults come with free food and lodging."

"I don't want to talk about cults!" I snapped at him.

"Fine," Kyle huffed. "Jesus. What's up your ass?"

"Apparently, lots and lots of coronavirus."

Kyle's eyes widened before he burst into a fit of hysterics. His laughter abruptly ended when he caught sight of my venomous glare. Kyle knew better than to rile me up, having weathered my violent, irrational outbursts for most of his life. Granted, this experience was bringing out the worst in me, and Kyle was the most convenient, no—*the only*—punching bag.

I did feel bad about taking my frustrations out on my brother, but there was nothing funny about the situation we found ourselves in. We were going on a month of isolation now, with no end in sight. And, the shitty part of it was that neither one of us was sick anymore. The virus, and all its symptoms, had passed through us two weeks ago. We both felt fine; yet the follow-up testing continued to show up positive.

"All I can say is, if we don't test negative this time around, I'm going to burn this place to the ground."

Okay, sure, that was a bit dramatic on my part, but I'd had all I could take. Three times the doctor had arrived to jam a footlong Q-tip into my brain, and twice he'd come back forty-eight hours later to deliver the unwelcome news. And now, here he was again, crossing over the pool deck on his way to the guest house to give us the results of the latest test. They say the third time's the charm. It had better be, or my parents would be dealing with their insurance company.

"What do you think?" I asked, standing at the window watching the doctor approach. "Does he look happy?"

"Who, Dr. Fry?" Kyle replied.

I turned my head to shoot daggers into his soul. "Do you see anybody else out there?"

"Oh." He shrugged. "I thought maybe you were talking about the unicorn pool floaty."

My eye began to twitch. I think... yes, it was official... *the* most irritating person on the planet had died, and now my brother wore the crown.

Between clenched teeth, I explained my previous question. "I meant, does Dr. Fry—not the unicorn pool floaty—look like he's about to deliver good news or bad?"

"He's wearing a hazmat suit, Jake. That's never a good sign."

"Dammit!" I roared, swinging the door open to the startled doc. "Let's just get this over with. Are we still positive, or not?"

The man spoke through the confines of his mask. "Jake, I'm pleased to tell you that you are free to go."

His words took a moment to register. I'd been waiting to hear Dr. Fry say that for so long, I honestly wasn't sure how to react. "Are you sure?"

"Yes. You tested negative for the virus."

"Oh, thank god," I blew out the breath I'd been holding before realization took hold. The doctor wasn't looking like he'd just emerged from a bat cave to deliver bad news to *me*. He was here for Kyle.

"What about my brother?" I asked.

Doctor Fry and Kyle exchanged a conspiratorial grin. I looked between the two. "Wait, what's going on? What am I missing?"

"May I?" the doc asked Kyle.

"Sure," he replied. "Go right ahead."

"Jake, Kyle tested negative two weeks ago. He was free to leave whenever he wanted."

I let the words sink into my brain. My god. He'd stayed locked in here... for me.

"Why?" I asked my brother, although I didn't need to hear the answer. I already knew. Kyle would do anything for me.

I didn't deserve him.

13

KENZIE

LOCKDOWN – DAY 30

"I THINK YOU MISSED YOUR CALLING, QUINN," I SAID TO MY brother-in-law, who was perched high up on a ladder, painting the second-floor exterior of the Scottish castle play-house that he'd insisted on buying for his nieces and neph-ews, to spruce up the McKallister's already ridiculously child-friendly backyard.

"At least I have something to fall back on if music doesn't work out," he said, smoothing more paint over the wood siding.

Quinn would not be needing a backup plan. With a string of hit songs, he'd already secured himself a place in history—and in my good graces. Younger than his siblings, I'd always considered Quinn the most elusive of the McKallister broth-ers, fading into the background of the big personalities that had propelled the famous family forward. For that reason, I'd never really felt much of a connection to him... until the pandemic hit, and suddenly, we all found ourselves living under the same roof.

With the other men of the household locked away in the

guest house, Quinn emerged from his own two-week quarantine as the only other male presence in the house besides Scott, and was instantly propelled into celebrity status amongst the kids. Filling the 'fun uncle' role effortlessly, it was not uncommon to see him swimming with his nieces and nephews in the pool or rolling around with them in the grass. But what I'd appreciated most was that he'd taken the time to sit down and chat with me. As it turned out, Quinn was every bit as personable as his older siblings, and I kicked myself for not having made the effort to connect with him sooner.

"And how did you say you were with Ikea furniture?" I asked.

"I didn't. I don't even try."

"It's not that bad." I laughed. "I'll have you know Kyle is a wizard when it comes to putting that stuff together."

"That doesn't surprise me. The directions are in a storybook form."

I laughed again. It was true. With Kyle, explanations had always gone easier with pictures. "How about I do the figuring out and you do the screwing?"

"Yes," he agreed, dazzling me with his smirk. "I'm good at screwing."

"Oh, I'm sure you are."

Before he could reply with more innuendo, Quinn glanced behind me while raising a hand to block out the sun. I saw his eyes widen.

"Sweet merciful crap!" he exclaimed. "They live."

I swung around, and like a slow-motion scene straight out of a movie, Kyle and Jake strolled across the grass toward us. There were a few moments in life that meant more than others, and this was definitely one of them. I'd been waiting a long time to see my man in the flesh, and now that he was here, I couldn't repress my high-pitched squeal as I ran to Kyle, flinging myself into his arms.

Grabbing his face, I planted a series of kisses on his lips. It was hard to describe how much I'd missed him. Kyle and I weren't one of those couples who needed space. We worked together. We played together. And we were raising two boys together. Kyle was my best friend in every sense of the word, and although I'd glommed on to his little brother in the interim, there was no substitute for the real thing.

"Oh man, Kenz, I can't tell you how happy I am to see your beautiful face. No offense to you, dude," Kyle said with a nod to Jake. "But I wasn't sure if I could take one more day of your ugly mug."

"Right back at ya," Jake replied, smiling as he moved past us with purpose.

"Oh, and Kenzie?" he called over his shoulder. "You've got yourself a good man—the best."

"I know," I answered back. Not a day passed that I wasn't thankful for the life I had. "You're not so bad yourself."

Jake raised his hand, receiving my words but not looking back. I knew exactly where he was headed: to Casey.

Turning back to Kyle, I mouthed, "He knows?"

Kyle nodded. "He does now."

I hugged my husband a little tighter, savoring the moment. Two weeks ago, I'd received a call from Kyle with the good news—he'd tested negative for the virus. But my joy was short-lived when, in the same breath, he'd told me that Jake had not. I knew before he even asked for my permission that Kyle wouldn't leave his brother. And no way was I going to ask him to, either. I'd known when I married Kyle that his loyalty to Jake was absolute. Sure, I could have demanded that he to return to us, but it would've pained him. So, as much as I wanted our little family reunited, I understood that this was something Kyle had to do.

"What about me?" Quinn asked, waiting for a similar compliment.

"You're a good man too," I said, flashing him a thumbs up.

Quinn tipped his head in thanks.

Kyle looked up, as if only just realizing his brother was up there on the ladder. "Dude, not cool. Put a shirt on around my wife."

Tossing me straight under the bus, Quinn replied, "She's the one who suggested I take it off."

Oh, boy. Thanks, jerk!

Employing the use of my big Bambi eyes, I spun an emergency web of damage control. "I suggested he take it off so he wouldn't get paint on his clothes," I explained. Very, very logical. And, while the whole paint angle wasn't a lie, I'd be remiss if I didn't admit Quinn was a sight for bored eyes.

"If that were the case, why isn't he totally naked then?" Kyle asked.

I bit down on my lower lip, cringing. "I didn't think I could get away with it."

Never one to hold a grudge, Kyle fought off a smile and said, "You get one communicable disease and suddenly your wife is undressing your baby brother."

I laughed, sidling up to my hubby. "Come on, Shaggy, you know I like my men pale, skinny, and goofy."

"Well then, lucky you." Kyle grinned, tucking his head into my neck and blowing raspberries. "I'm your dream come true."

Grabbing onto Kyle's shirt, I dragged him toward the castle door. "You have no idea. Come on. Let's play Outlander in the castle. You be Jaime."

"I have no idea what you just said," Kyle said. "But I'm digging the tone of voice."

"Oh, my god," Quinn panicked, scrambling down the rungs. "Let me at least get off the ladder first."

14

CASEY

"Slater, watch your sister a second while I help Miles with his homework."

Just the fact that I found nothing alarming with that sentence proved how far I'd come as a single mom since the lockdown began. Four weeks ago, tasking three-year-old Slater with any more responsibility than popping a pacifier into Lily's mouth would have seemed inconceivable. Now, I had the kid actively keeping her alive. How times had changed. Of course, it wasn't like Slater was going to be alone with her. I was right here checking Miles' work. I mean, how far could Lily get on her hands and knees?

Bending over Miles' shoulder, my eyes rounded in wonder as I scanned his writing assignment. He'd been tasked with writing something he liked about his kindergarten teacher. The prompts were all there for him, and all he needed to do was choose words from the provided list and fill them into the underlined blanks. *Ms. Stout is a good teacher. She is smart. I like when she does meth with us.*

I burst out laughing.

"What?" Miles asked, a quizzical expression on his face. Because he was such a meticulous child, he took his homework seriously, and clearly didn't appreciate me laughing at his efforts.

"Sorry, honey," I said, smoothing down his hair and kissing his head. "It looks good. You just misspelled math."

Before he could correct his work, I snapped a shot of it with my phone. It wasn't every day we got priceless material to add to the scrapbook, and I knew his daddy needed a laugh as much as I did.

"Mommy, Lily is a kitty," Slater announced proudly.

My middle child loved make-believe. He was always dressing up in costumes and was never without his trusty plastic sword. If he was pretending his sister was a cat, there was absolutely nothing out of the ordinary about that.

"I bet she's a pretty kitty," I replied, flipping the page in Miles' workbook.

"Yes," my middle child agreed. "She goes potty in the litter box too."

Mother of God! My heart dropped out of my chest. I already knew where my baby was without even looking her way. The McKallisters had a cat-sized door off the kitchen that led out to a fully enclosed kitty condo with wall-to-ceiling windows overlooking the backyard. Inside the feline paradise were climbing platforms, toys, and an oversized litterbox large enough to accommodate their three cats—and my nine-month-old daughter.

"Slater!" I screamed, racing to the window and peering through the glass at my precious baby girl squealing as she cast fistfuls of litter into the air. "What have you done?"

"She wanted to play with the kitties," he explained, his bottom lip already quivering.

"How'd you even get her in there?" I asked, although I already knew the answer. He'd pushed her big ol' diapered rump through the itty-bitty kitty door—of course.

Slater swayed in place, his expression unbalanced, as anger and embarrassment took hold. I had three... no, two seconds before the glass-shattering shrieks began. But when he opened his mouth to scream, no sound escaped him. I grabbed for my son but was not quick enough as his skin paled to a deathly white, his lips turned blue, and he collapsed to the floor.

"Michelle!" I screamed, scooping Slater's limp body up into my arms. I knew what to do because I'd been in this situation many times before. Sticking my finger into his mouth, I checked for an obstruction before determining that my middle child was, once again, suffering from a breath-holding spell. See, Slater had always been a hotbed of emotion, feeling everything to extremes. When he was happy, there was no one happier. When he was sad, the world cried with him, and when he was angry or embarrassed, my dramatic son held his breath and passed himself out.

Michelle rounded the corner just as I blew into Slater's face. He jerked, his arms splaying out before taking a breath. That was when the screaming started. With him in my arms, I slid to the floor, exhausted and relieved but also angry with myself for putting Slater... and me... into the situation in the first place. I knew better. What happened to the mother I'd always thought myself to be?

"Is he okay?" Michelle asked, running her fingers over the swelling already forming on his sweaty forehead.

I nodded, still too traumatized to explain. Instead, I tipped my head in the direction of the kitty condo and simply said, "Lily."

———

Forty minutes later, Miles had completed his homework, Lily was changed and bathed, and Slater had mercifully cried himself to sleep. Days like this were not in the brochure. They were also a reminder of how fortunate I was to have a part-time nanny to pick up the slack where I was clearly lacking. There was nothing like a little leveling of the playing field to knock one back down to size. Before the virus, before Jake fell ill, I'd prided myself on having it all: holding down a part-time job while raising three kids and attending glittery social events with my hot hubs. But the truth was, I did it all with help. Without it, I was the mom who set her kid up to fail and who had, quite possibly, introduced her daughter to a full-fledged furry fetish in her later years.

Ugh. Right about now, I wished I had Slater's superpower. How nice would it be to escape the scrutiny of a job poorly done by holding my breath and passing clean out onto the floor.

"Casey," Michelle said, grabbing my hand and squeezing, "you need a breather."

"No, I'm fine."

"No, you're not. Go take a break. Get a shower; maybe a nap. Scott and I have the kids."

"Are you sure?"

"Yes. Go."

"Okay. And if Lily gets a hairball, don't worry, she'll just hack it back up."

Michelle laughed and then wrapped her arms around me and gave me the hug I sorely needed. "You're a good mama, Casey. We all have bad days."

"I just... I feel like I'm failing Slater. I'm worried something is wrong."

"There's nothing wrong with him, Casey. He's his father's son. And those mighty lungs of his will one day carry him across a stage. Mark my words, Slater's going to be a star."

I STOOD in front of the mirror, my soiled clothing telling the story of my day. Snot, cat poop, and tears all conspiring to ruin my day. I had to let it go. Michelle was right. We all had bad days. Stripping off my clothes, I stepped into the shower and let the water rain down over my head. When had life gotten so rough around the edges? The virus, and the changes we'd had to make to accommodate it, was nothing in comparison to losing Jake. I needed him back. He was the missing link—the crunchy peanut butter to my messy jelly. Closing my eyes, I pressed my head to the glass and let the tears come. I wasn't sure how long I'd been drowning myself in my watery pity party when the shower door suddenly swung open and my husband was standing before me.

"Jake?"

Flinging off his shoes and tossing his phone onto the vanity, Jake stepped into the shower fully clothed and gathered me into his arms, holding me tighter than I think he ever had. Every bit of my anxiety and stress washed away in his strong embrace.

I gripped some of his sopping t-shirt into my hand and tugged. "You're such a nut. You couldn't take your clothes off first?"

"There was no time. You needed me."

Those words. His heart. I knew then everything was going to be all right. I reached up on my tip-toes and kissed him. "Yes, I needed you."

Jake trailed a finger over my breast. "I need you too."

"Tell me this is over, Jake."

"It's over."

"How can you be sure?"

"Because I'm smart and I do meth with my teacher."

"You got the picture?"

"Oh, I got the picture, all right."

"Can you imagine if I hadn't caught that? The teacher would've checked the name and been like, 'Oh right, the McKallister boy. His dad's a rock star. They probably bathe in the stuff.'"

"I think you should have just let him turn it in. I don't want to be the kind of parent who has to rush in and save my kid. I want him to make mistakes. That's what life is all about. Look how many mistakes I've made, and I'm still ticking."

"Yes, but you're superhuman. The rest of us aren't as bulletproof."

"And that's why I'm here to protect you."

I gripped his chin between my fingers and looked him in the eyes, repeating my earlier question. "How can you be sure you're all right?"

"I tested negative, Casey. I'm free—unlike my daughter, who you imprisoned in cat jail."

A smile jumped freely to my face, finally finding some humor in the afternoon from hell. "Ah, you heard that, huh?"

"I heard a lot of things." Jake laughed. "And might I add, that was some stellar parenting there, champ."

"Well, you know. I've always been an out of the box kind of gal."

"Yes, you have. It's what I love about you."

"And your mom made me feel better about Slater. She said, with his lungs and his temperament, he was going to be just like his daddy."

Jake wrapped his arms around my waist. "God help him."

"I don't know." I reached down and pulled his sopping shirt over his head and tossed it to the floor of the shower. "I say he should be so lucky."

"That's only because you're biased," he replied, his hands cupping my ass and squeezing.

My fingers fumbled with his jeans, now vacuum-sealed to his body and held down by twenty pounds of water weight. "At least you could have taken these off before getting in to save me."

"I was going for romantic," he said, dipping his head into the hollows of my neck and kissing me all while unbuttoning his pants and sliding them over his waist and legs.

I stepped back, looking at him. Even though he'd lost some weight in quarantine, I couldn't remember ever seeing him as sexy as he was now, water sliding through his hair and down the rugged body, marked with scars and etched with tattoos, that I loved so much. Jake lay his head against the glass as I traced my fingers over his slick stomach and then grabbed hold.

"Have you been saving yourself for me?" I whispered.

"Um..." he hesitated, a charming grin falling over his handsome face. "Sure."

I laughed, feeling light and free for the first time since he'd gone away. Everything was going to be all right again. I could feel it in my bones.

"What about you?" he asked, slipping his fingers down and brushing them between my legs.

"Sure," I groaned. Jake kept the pressure up as mini explosions rocked through me. "But nothing feels as good as you."

Placing my hand against his chest, I pushed him back against the glass. He didn't need any prompting, already hard and wanting. Jake lifted me off the ground and my legs wrapped around him. Keeping my eyes focused on him as he entered me, I crushed my lips to his and savored the feel of his body sealed in mine. His capable hands holding me steady, I set the rhythm—slow and steady at first, but as the heat burned through me, I increased the intensity until he was driving deeper inside. Hitting a crescendo, I buried my head in his neck to stifle the screams as my man carried me off to oblivion.

Returning me to wobbly legs, Jake slid his fingers into my wet hair and pulled me toward him, dropping a kiss to my forehead then moving over the rest of my face. He'd missed me, like I had him. It occurred to me then why I'd been so off lately. Jake and I were never meant to survive alone. Michelle might not have known then, but when she was raising Jake, she was molding him into the man I would someday love. My thoughts shifted to Slater. I would do the same for him – shape him into the best version I could before offering him up to a lucky someone.

"You good?" Jake asked, tipping up my chin and pressing a gentle kiss to my lips.

I nodded, smiling up at him as my strength returned. "I'm great."

"Let's go home."

EPILOGUE: KEITH

LOCKDOWN – DAY 55

"You're late," Jake said, intercepting me in the driveway.

"Yeah, well, it was somewhat unavoidable given the circumstances," I grumbled, readjusting the suit I'd hastily thrown on in my bid to get out the door. Either I'd gained a few pounds during quarantine or someone had snuck into my house while I was eating and snipped an inch or two off the waistband. Or maybe it was just that I wasn't used to actual clothes restricting my body anymore. The great part of owning a surf shop was that the wardrobe requirements were minimal. My work uniform consisted mainly of board shorts and tank tops. Or, if I was feeling a little more formal, pocket shorts and a t-shirt. Then the pandemic hit, and Sam was lucky to find me in anything more substantial than a pair of boxers.

"Did Sam and the boys make it?" I asked.

"Yes. They're here. Everyone's here. We've all just been waiting on you."

What was new? I'd never been the most punctual guy.

Why give the most important job of the day to me? What were they thinking?

"I'm here. Chill out, dude."

"I would, except..." Jake's mouth twitched like it wanted to say something but was worried I might punch it if it did.

"Except what?" I asked, impatiently.

"Okay, don't get all pissed off, but I gotta ask. Did you get caught in a hurricane on the way over here?"

"What do you mean?" My hands shot to my head. "Oh, shit!"

My hair. I knew I'd forgotten something. No surprise, given what I'd been dealing with all morning. Sam and I had awoken to a bang. It took all of two minutes to discover the burst water heater in the garage. Typically, such a thing would have been an unwelcome headache, but given that half of our covid-closed store's merchandise was stacked floor to ceiling in the watery hell, it became a race against time to get our livelihood onto dry land.

"No offense, Keith, but you look like a lounge singer who's been throwing up all night."

"Yeah, well you look like..." I let my words run dry after getting a peek at my brother and finding absolutely nothing to insult him on. In fact, he looked like a fucking runway model in his fitted designer suit. It even looked like... yes, the asshole had somehow gotten a haircut in the middle of a pandemic.

Jake continued with his unhelpful commentary. "You might want to fix it because there will be pictures."

Like I didn't understand the situation. I knew full well what today entailed. It wasn't like my hair was actively trying to derail the proceedings. "Do you have a comb or something?"

He raised a brow. "A weed whacker might be of more benefit."

"Jake! You're not helping," I snapped back. "Get me a damn comb, now!"

"Jesus. So testy," he said, checking his watch as he jogged up the stairs. "Follow me."

We raced into the house and straight to the nearest bathroom. As I scoured through the drawers for something – anything – Jake ran off in another direction to try his luck. He returned a minute later with a brush in his hand.

I raised a brow. "Tell me that's not what I think it is."

"It's all I could find," he panted, offering it up to me. "Take it or leave it."

"If I take it, are you going to tell anyone what happened here today?"

Jake thought about it a moment before giving me an honest reply. "Yes."

Of course he was.

I nodded. "Fair enough."

Grabbing the dog brush, I raked it through my rowdy hair.

JAKE and I exited the bathroom together, and while normally the optics of that might have warranted an off-color joke directed at my brother, neither one of us was in the mood for a bit of light-hearted word play. On our way out the door, we ran straight-on into Grace.

"Keith!"

That one word encompassed so many different emotions. Anger, frustration, impatience.

Jake dipped out of the conversation before it even began. "I've got to go find Quinn."

Really? He was just leaving me on the rocky ridge to die? This was no band of brothers.

Grace and I watched him walk away before she turned back to me, hand on hip.

I swallowed, actually somewhat fearful of what she had to say. Wait a minute! Why was I scared of my baby sister? What was she... like, twelve?

"Grace!" I mimicked back... to show her who was boss.

"Do you remember our conversation?" she asked, as if speaking to a child.

I remembered. She'd called last night before bed. In fact, she'd called every night before bed for the last week. But then, I supposed I could cut her some slack since my little sister was the brains behind this operation. Three weeks ago, she'd come up with the idea to surprise our parents for their thirty-fifth wedding anniversary, and since the entire family was homebound in Los Angeles for the unforeseeable future, we all just fell in line behind her like dutiful little soldiers.

"No," I lied.

"No?" The edge in her voice told me Gracie was no longer a child. What year was she born again? I calculated her age in my head while she waited. And waited.

"Holy shit! Are you twenty-one years old?"

"Twenty-two," she sighed. "Focus, Keith. You promised to be here an hour in advance to go over your speaking parts."

I wasn't paying attention, still focused on how she'd

grown up without me noticing. "Damn, you're way older than I thought."

"Keith!"

Another one-word accusation. Damn, she had more Emma in her than I realized.

"Relax, Gracie-Bear," I said, patting her head. "I already have my speaking parts memorized. I've got this."

MOVING AWAY FROM MY SISTER-BOSS, I slipped into the kitchen to get a quick snack when I ran into Emma. Her assigned job was the food, and damned if she wasn't taking it seriously. The counter was full of covered platters.

"Ah, look who the cat dragged in." Emma smirked as she got a full-body look at me. "You look just lovely. I really like the Labradoodle hair. Very stylish."

"Jake told you *already*?" I gaped. "When does he find the time to tattle?"

Emma smiled. "Some people accomplish things before noon, Keith. It's called an alarm clock."

"I accomplish things. For example, I have four boxes of bikinis now drying in the sun."

Emma cringed. "Yeah, Sam told me about that. Were you able to save any of your merchandise?"

"Yeah, only the boxes on the garage floor were affected, but they were all wrapped in plastic, so I think it's fine."

"That's good. And Jake didn't rush in here to snitch. I was in the kitchen when he found the dog brush."

"Why would mom keep the dog brush in the kitchen in the first place?"

Emma pointed toward the back wall. "Probably for the same reason she has a cat condo off the picture window."

Quinn came sliding into the room. "Has anyone seen Jake?"

"He just took off. He was looking for you."

"Oh!" Quinn startled. "Is he pissed?"

Why Quinn assumed he was in trouble, I had no idea, but now that I knew he did, I couldn't pass up the opportunity to mess with him. I mean, what kind of a big brother would I be if I didn't get that blood of his pumping a little faster?

"Well, he didn't look happy," I warned. "Like on a scale from one to ten—I'd say he was maybe an eleven."

"Seriously?" Quinn groaned. "I don't know why he's mad at me. You're the one that's late. And..." Quinn scanned me with his eyes like all of my other siblings had, and like them, he also managed to find fault.

"Uh, Keith. Are you... um... planning on wearing those flip-flops with your suit?"

I followed his eyes down, wiggling my toes. The original plan had been to dig my dress shoes out of the hall closet, but in my haste to get over here, I'd forgotten. It wasn't until I was pulling into the driveway that I realized I was still wearing my beach thongs.

"Yeah. You got a problem with that?" I asked, puffing my chest to project importance. Afterall, I was still his superior, even though his bank account might say otherwise.

Quinn lifted his hands to placate me. "Hey, I don't have a problem. But Mom might."

"Mom?" I waved off his concerns. "She hasn't approved of anything I've worn since I was ten. Besides, it's just family. Who's going to judge me?"

Maybe if we were expecting a crowd, I might have put more effort into my appearance, but here at home, surrounded by my loved ones, why try? If anyone would be okay with ingrown toenails, it would be them. That was the beauty of family.

AT GRACE'S INSISTENCE, I headed outside to take my place on the platform, passing Kyle along the way. He'd been put in charge of decorations and was hanging lights along the white fencing.

"Hey," I said, bumping fists with my little bro.

"Hey, dude. What's up?"

"Not much," I replied, my eyes widening as they took in Kyle's stylistic choices. "What do we have here?"

Kyle shrugged. "The decorations."

"Huh. Has Grace seen these?"

"No. It's a surprise."

I nodded. Oh yes, this would be a surprise, all right. I ran my fingers along the string lights.

"Are these... tacos?"

"Yeah. Grace said to order something fun and whimsical. What's more festive than tacos?"

I gripped his shoulder. It was more consolatory than anything else. Once Grace got a load of this, Kyle would be on life support, so there was no point in ruining what was left of his day.

"I like it. Oh, and don't forget to hang that giant blowup chalupa over by the alter."

. . .

STANDING front and center in my too-tight suit, poufy hair, and flip-flopped feet, I watched as my mother made her way down the aisle, flowers in hand, flanked by her daughters—all of them—Emma, Grace, Casey, Kenzie, Sam, and Kate. My dad stood on the stage beside me, with his sons—all of then —Me, Mitch, Jake, Finn, Kyle, and Quinn.

The only ones left in the audience were the grandkids, the youngest ones being tended to by the oldest. This wasn't a big celebratory affair. It wasn't even a small one. This was just family, coming together to honor our own. Thirty-five years of love and struggle. Thirty-five years of laughter and tears. They'd survived it all. But the one thing they'd never done together was walk down the aisle—until today.

Left to their own accord, my parents would've never renewed their vows. They'd always been fine with their bare-bones nuptials at the city hall, attended only by her sister and his brother. They didn't need pomp and circumstance to prove their love for one another... or their commitment. They just needed each other... and us.

So, in keeping with that family first approach, my parents had planned a vacation to Hawaii to celebrate their thirty-fifth anniversary and invited all of us to come. But then the virus hit, tipping the world upside down. With their trip canceled, my parents had, no doubt, resigned themselves to a quiet evening alone... until we all began arriving a little over an hour ago. It was only then that they realized something unexpected was happening. Still, they couldn't have predicted this – an altar set up in their backyard and a chance for my mom to finally walk down the aisle and marry the man she loved.

Mom arrived at the platform stage looking radiant in one

of the dresses her daughters had picked out for her. She was the first woman I'd ever loved, and I credited her with giving me the heart I'd needed to love my own wife and kids. I cleared my throat, fighting back the emotion, as I spoke my first words.

"We are gathered here today..."

My siblings had given me the honor of 'marrying' our parents. And, despite what my appearance might say about me, I'd taken my job seriously, even going so far as to get my minister's certificate from an online church. No, I wasn't really marrying them – that job had been done by a justice of the peace thirty-five years ago – but I didn't want to let them down either. My parents had sacrificed so much for us, and it was the least my brothers and sisters could do—to make them feel special and loved on this notable day.

After speaking for a few minutes, I turned the spotlight on my brothers. Jake and Quinn, sitting off to the side with guitars in hand, began their moving rendition of "Time in a Bottle." The song, speaking to timeless love, was more than appropriate, given the history of the couple it was honoring. This was a celebration of life and love, but it was also a memory of the struggle and what we'd all collectively survived.

As the final, heart-wrenching lines were sung, there wasn't a dry eye in the place. But then, every single person in attendance had a vested interest in this couple. They were the link that connected us all. Family was only as strong as its core... and ours was solid steel.

"And by the power vested in me by UniversalLifeChurch.-com, I now pronounce you man and wife."

The End

BONUS MATERIAL

Want to get to know the Cake clan a little better? Maybe discover some never before revealed secrets of this famous family? For the first time ever a reporter is allowed inside the McKallister home to get up close and personal with these larger-than-life characters.

CASEY

Interviewer: How honest are you?

Casey: Honest? Oh, wow. Okay, well, are you asking like on a scale from one to ten?

Interviewer: Sure.

Casey: I'd say maybe a six.

Interviewer: Just a six?

Casey: Why? Is that low? You know what, can I change my answer to a seven? I feel like I'm kind of in between the two numbers, so it makes sense to round up, don't you think?

Interviewer: Makes sense. What was the last lie you told?

Casey: (*whispers*) Is Jake here?

Interviewer: I think he's in the other room.

Casey: Oh, whew, okay, good. My last lie was this morning. So we have this dog, and he's always going out back and eating grass, but then when he comes in, he throws up on the floor. Jake and I have an agreement that whoever sees it first has to pick it up. Let's just say, when Jake's home, I *never* see it.

JAKE

Interviewer: What was your most memorable fan encounter?

Jake: Oh, man, I've had a few. One time these two girls come up to me and they're really excited, but one of them is shaking so hard her teeth are knocking together... then bam! Down she goes. Just passes out cold. I was with a couple of bandmates at the time, and as we were trying to revive her, the girl's friend just kept chattering on like nothing happened – totally unconcerned. It was the weirdest thing. I felt like I was in the *Twilight Zone*.

Interviewer: Was she okay?

Jake: Yeah, she woke up and wanted a selfie. And there was another memorable one a couple of years ago. I boarded a plane and took my seat. The woman sitting beside me looked up briefly from her phone, gave me a slight smile of acknowledgment, and then went back to her screen. I was thinking, 'Sweet, she either doesn't know who I am or doesn't care. This will be an easy flight.' So we took off and were in the air for about an hour. The flight attendants had already served drinks and everything. Suddenly I heard this loud gasp, and when I turned toward the woman, she was gaping at me with these wide, disbelieving eyes and said, "When did you get here?"

KENZIE

Interviewer: Do you believe in Bigfoot?

Kenzie: Did Kyle put you up to this?

Interviewer: He might have suggested a few interview questions.

Kenzie: Of course he did. Okay, so here's the deal, I'm not saying I believe in Bigfoot, even though he has a museum and all, but I know people who swear to have seen him, and they're all fairly sane individuals... well, except for Dumpster Dirk. He once carried around a dead raccoon strapped to his chest with duct tape for a whole week, so... yeah... I can't really swear by his eyewitness account. Oh, and Vanessa. She's not all that believable either, what with the whole fake pregnancy thing. Otherwise, the rest of them are very trustworthy.

Interviewer: Have you ever seen him yourself?

Kenzie: Heck, no. I'm not a psycho. Can you ask me a real question, please?

Interviewer: How many times have you watched *Blue Lagoon*?

Kenzie: KYLE!

KYLE

Interviewer: What's it like having a rock star for a brother?

Kyle: It sucks because people are always asking me what it's like to have a rock star for a brother. Ask me something else. I want a fun question.

Interviewer: Fun? Okay, would you rather fight a horse-sized duck or 100 duck-sized horses?

Kyle: Ha! That's what I'm talking about! I'd rather fight a horse-sized duck, of course.

Interviewer: Why?

Kyle: Have you ever seen an angry duck? I haven't. And even if the duck spent some time in the gym pumpin' iron and gettin' juiced, at the end of the day, it's still a daffy little duck. What's the worst it could do – demand an entire loaf of bread instead of a few breadcrumbs? Speaking of ducks, here's a fun fact. I didn't know ducks could fly until I was on the reality show *Marooned*.

Interviewer: Really? How did you think they got from one place to another?

Kyle: That's the thing – I'd only ever seen ducks hanging out on lakes or ponds. I just assumed they walked or floated everywhere.

EMMA

Interviewer: Rate how useful your siblings would be in a zombie apocalypse.

Emma: Let's start with Grace. She's scrappier than she looks, but take away her phone and she's as helpless as a newborn baby. She wouldn't rank higher than a two. Quinn, he's always got something to prove, so I'm confident he could fight his way through a herd of undead just to show up his brothers. I give him an eight.

Interviewer: And Kyle?

Emma: He'd be the first to die.

Interviewer: Why?

Emma: Have you met him? He thinks he can fight a horse-sized duck with a loaf of bread. I think that speaks for itself. He ranks a one.

Interviewer: What about Jake?

Emma: Jake's the ultimate survivor. He's like the weed that grows out of the sidewalk. You can chop him down to the roots, but he'll rise again. If there's a zombie apocalypse, mark my words – Jake will be the last man standing. He scores a ten.

And that takes us to Keith. He's a tricky one for sure. See, Keith's the kind of guy who can't fight worth crap but can talk his way out of anything. Problem is, zombies aren't known for their communication skills. So I think if he hid behind Jake or Quinn and made it to a safe zone, Keith could eventually become their leader. So, I'd give him a seven.

Interviewer: And you?

Emma: Me? Oh no, I don't do zombies.

FINN

Interviewer: You seem very comfortable with the McKallisters. Are they similar to your own family?

Finn: (*laughs*) Oh, wait. Were you being serious?

Interviewer: Yes, why?

Finn: It's just the McKallister family is the polar opposite of the one I grew up in. Michelle and Scott are hands-on. My mother believed in free-range parenting, sort of like that mother on the news recently who left her young kids at home to fend for themselves while she went on vacation to Germany. My mother, Shelby, would have been the first one on that plane if she'd had the money for a ticket. And you know what? I probably wouldn't have noticed she was gone.

Interviewer: So I take it you prefer the hands-on approach.

Finn: I just like the whole family feel. Do you know the McKallisters have a family group text where they talk about their day, share funny stories, and post raunchy pictures? If the Perry family had a group chat, it would need a PayPal link.

KEITH

Interviewer: Name your favorite family memory.

Keith: Ah, yes. You've come to the right person. I've got a good one for you, but my mother has forbidden the retelling of this story outside of the family unit. So I'm going to talk quietly (*lowers his voice*). When I was probably around fifteen, my family went to an amusement park. We spent the whole day there, and my dad was getting tired and cranky, so after dinner he was ready to go. We managed to sweet talk our mom into letting us go on one more ride, but by the time it was over, both Jake and Kyle were feeling queasy. We hadn't been driving for more than ten minutes when Kyle threw up out the window. That set Jake off, but unfortunately, he was in the middle seat. My dad was forced to make an emergency stop to kick the boys out. He was already pissed, and now he was cleaning up puke. Anyway, the rest of us in the backseat took a direct hit, and since we weren't that far from home, my mom had us take off our soiled clothes, stripped to our underwear. While Dad was cleaning up and Mom was tending to the boys, Emma got out because the smell was getting to her.

Interviewer: I'm already not liking where this is going.

Keith: Oh, wait, it gets better. It was dark out and Emma couldn't see where she was going. Suddenly she screamed, "Something bit me." Turns out she backed into a cactus, and the spines went straight through her underwear and buried themselves in her right butt cheek and the back of her leg. Every time she tried to swipe at them, the thorns transferred onto her hands. Emma was literally covered in hundreds of these little cactus spines and had to hold her hands out like Wolverine. My poor mom now had two pukers, three queasy kids, and one porcupine. She just lost it; laughed so hard she peed her pants, forcing her to undress with the rest of us. So there we were, all stripped down to our skivvies, with Emma lying over our laps because she couldn't sit down. We were five miles from home when my father was pulled over for speeding.

SAMANTHA (SAM)

Interviewer: If you could change one thing about Keith, what would it be?

Sam: Oh, you're trying to get me in trouble, aren't you? Okay, there is one thing I would change. Keith has an obsession with sauce. Everything has to be dipped, dripped, or drowned.

Interviewer: Can you give us an example?

Sam: Well, he's got his standard pasta dishes, which I get. But Keith takes it that extra step further. In his own words, the 'wetter the better.' He dips his pizza in ranch, his veggies in ketchup, his fruit in peanut butter.
You want to know how to ruin Keith's day? Gyp him on his ranch packets in the drive-thru. The other day the poor guy only got one dipping sauce with his 20-piece nuggets and had to ration it like it was World War Two.

Interviewer: Sounds like Keith has a junk food habit.

Sam: Oh, yes. I try to have healthy choices for the family and limit sweets in the house. A couple of years ago, I found his secret stash. He hides it in the very top cupboard of the pantry, in a green plastic bin. It's stocked full of Gummy Worms and Oreos and Frito Lays.

Interviewer: What did you do with this damning information?

Sam: Are you kidding? I shut the cupboard and walked away. Where else am I going to get my sweet and salty fix?

QUINN

Interviewer: Do you have any irrational fears?

Quinn: I'm afraid of airplane toilets... and mayonnaise. I admit airplane toilets are probably a dumb fear. I mean what are the chances of being sucked through that tiny hole and spit out into the sky? Probably pretty small.

Interviewer: Actually, I think the chances are zero. Are you afraid of all toilets or just airplane ones?

Quinn: I'm not going to lie; the automatic toilets freak me out too. Like, if it flushes before I'm done, I'll pinch it off and get the hell out of there.

Interviewer: What scares you about mayonnaise?

Quinn: Dude, I can't even... it's like the devil to me. The way it wiggles and the sticky sound it makes. (*shivers*)

Interviewer: So, I take it deviled eggs are out of the question?

Quinn: Oh, yeah. If I see food sticking together with something white, I automatically assume the worst.

Interviewer: Do you have any idea where this fear comes from?

Quinn: I'm the youngest of five boys... where do you think it comes from? One time, at Christmas, we were frosting cookies, and Mom called me away for some reason. When I arrived back in the kitchen, my brothers gave me a cookie with frosting and sprinkles and told me to eat it. I had a bad feeling because they were a little too eager, if you know what I mean. I refused, but they wouldn't take no for an answer. They held me down and forced it into my mouth.

Interviewer: Let me guess, it was frosted with mayonnaise.

Quinn: Yep. And since then, I can't even carry the jar to the refrigerator. Actually, I have a third irrational fear... my brothers.

GRACE

Interviewer: Being the youngest sibling, do you find yourself always competing for attention?

Grace: Not really. Quinn and I were pretty self-sufficient. Plus, the older ones were all out of the house by the time we hit double digits. But I've always loved having a big family and am super proud of my older siblings. And being the baby has its perks.

Interviewer: Like?

Grace: Well, for example, I was watching PG-13 movies when I was two. Keith didn't get a phone until he was seventeen. I had one when I was eleven. The only thing I don't like is automatically being relegated to the backseat. I feel like once everyone reaches 18-years-old, we should all be on a level playing field.

Interviewer: Growing up, what did kids at school think about Jake being your brother?

Grace: (*laughs*) It was an adventure, for sure. One time when I was in middle school, my parents had to go out of town with Quinn for a music exhibition. Emma was supposed to watch me, but she got sick at the last minute, and the only one available to pick me up from school was Jake. I mean, when it gets to Jake, you know the entire chain of available siblings has been completely exhausted. Anyway, that day I'd accidentally left my phone at home, so I had no idea he was coming to get me. I was looking for Emma's car, not his, so after aggressively trying to get my attention by honking like a lunatic, he was finally forced to get out the car and come find me. As soon as they saw him coming, the entire student body started screaming, just totally freaking out. It was like a One Direction concert in the parking lot. And then, to make matters worse, Jake had to take me to the Nike store to get new basketball shoes and then go with me to my first practice that night. I didn't learn a thing because no one could concentrate on basketball. No lie... there was a lot of mania and weeping going on that day.

SCOTT

Interviewer: Tell me about your kids.

Scott: They're jerks... every single one of them. The only one I half-way like is (*pauses*)... no, never mind, I don't like her either.

Interviewer: (*laughs*) Why don't you like them?

Scott: I'll tell you why. I used to be a cool guy – the long-haired surfer dude. The kickass mailman rocking the snazzy little shorts. I was strutting around like a peacock. We're talking sky-high self-esteem. And then I had kids. Suddenly everything I did was (*finger quotes*) 'embarrassing.' Bunch of ingrates, if you ask me. Do you see anything wrong with bowling shirts? Of course you don't, because they're epic. Yet every one of my kids mocked me for it when I came downstairs. They made me change clothes.

'Bowling shirts are all the rage,' I said.

'In the 1950s,' they answered.

I wasn't even born in the 50's. Jerks! And then, at lunch, they made fun of the way I ate carrots. Carrots! I mean if there's a quiet way to eat carrots, by all means, educate me.

Interviewer: Is there anything you like about your kids?

Scott: I like when they go home.

MICHELLE

Interviewer: I asked your husband this same question. Tell me about your kids.

Michelle: They're just amazing. Smart, kind, generous. I'm so proud of the wonderful people they've become.

Interviewer: Huh, yeah, a little different than your husband's answer. Do you have a favorite child?

Michelle: Absolutely not. I love them all equally. I guess you could say they're all my favorites.

Keith: (*Interrupts the interview*) But if we were all dangling off a cliff and you could only save one of us, who would it be?

Michelle: Why would you all be dangling off a cliff?

Keith: I don't know. Maybe there was an earthquake. Just answer the question.

Michelle: You know I'm not going to answer that, Keith.

Keith: So, you'd just let us all die? Is that what you're saying? Great parenting.

Michelle: No, what I'm saying is no loving mother can answer a question like that. It's like that game you always make me play where you give me the most impossible choices, like "Would you rather be aggressively punched in the gut by Mike Tyson or sleep in a bed of spiders?" News flash, Keith, I don't want either.

Keith: That's the point of the game. The choices have to be hard. Answer this one and I'll leave you alone about your poor parenting choices.

Michelle: Fine.

Keith: Would you rather start every conversation for the rest of your life with the phrase, "I'm wearing a diaper" or not know the difference between a baby and a muffin?

Michelle: (*long pause*) I'd let you drop.

THE CAKE SERIES

Cake A Love Story is the first book in the Cake series. Every McKallister sibling was affected by the tragedy that rocked their family and all still struggle with the aftermath as adults. If you only read Cake, you will miss essential parts of the story as new information about, not only the kidnapping, but also the family is fleshed out in each subsequent book. Of course, every Cake story has its own unique love story to enjoy as well.

In book two, The Theory of Second Best, you will learn what happened the day Jake disappeared and why Kyle harbors such feelings of guilt. You will also get a fun, lively friends-to-lovers story set on an island with a cast of lovable characters.

In book three, Fiercely Emma, you will go back in time to learn what happened to the family during the month Jake went missing. Follow along with the McKallisters as they struggle to help teenage Jake heal from the crime that nearly ended his life. You will also get a present day opposites-attract love story set at a music festival. Emma just might be the most misunderstood McKallister. This book is her redemption.

In book four, Cake: The Newlyweds, Jake and Casey are back with new adventures and fresh struggles. As always, their story will be told with love, laughter, and a touch of heartache.

And, in book five, Rogue Wave, travel all the way back to a time never before explored in the McKallister saga and see what life was like *before* tragedy took the members of this family out at the knees. You will also get an entertaining opposites attract, second chance love story that spans over a decade.

Up Next? Quinn's story.

ABOUT THE AUTHOR

J. (Jill) Bengtsson is the bestselling author of the Cake Series. She writes contemporary novels focused on love, humor, passion, and family. Her heroines are strong, nurturing, and quirky while her heroes are what dreams are made of - gorgeous, committed, and in need of a little saving. A native Californian, Jill's novels are set under the glittering lights of the West Coast entertainment industry. They are for the dreamer in all of us.

Jill resides in Ventura County, California. She's married to the Swedish boy she met as an exchange student her junior year in college and they have three children, a golden retriever, and two ragdoll cats.

J. Bengtsson is represented by Michelle Wolfson of the Wolfson Literary Agency. All foreign rights inquiries can be directed toward Taryn Fagerness.

Never miss a release! Sign up for Jill's mailing list and stay up to date on what is happening in the Cake world and beyond. https://jbengtssonbooks.com/newsletter

———

*If you enjoyed this story, please consider leaving a review to

share your experience with other readers. Hunker Down with the McKallisters: A Cake Series Novella.

Want a more interactive experience? Join The Banana Binder, a place dedicated to the characters who've come to love.

www.jbengtssonbooks.com
Jill@jbengtssonbooks.com

Made in the USA
Coppell, TX
28 October 2020

40387928R00073